"What happens now?"

His hand lingered a moment, his fingers warm against her jawline. "We're going to a safe house."

"We?"

"You and me."

"Oh."

He cocked his head. "Is that a problem?"

She shook her head. "No. No problem."

Except it was. It was a huge problem. It was hard enough getting over her lingering feelings for her boss when she passed him in the hallway at Cooper Security three or four times a week.

How was she supposed to move on with her life stuck in a safe house with him 24/7?

PAULA GRAVES

SECRET INTENTIONS

HARLEQUIN®

entertain, enrich, inspire™

For my Aunt Marie, one of my most avid fans. I love you.

Recycling programs
for this product may
not exist in your area.

ISBN-13: 978-0-373-74699-6

SECRET INTENTIONS

www.Harlequin.com

Printed in U.S.A.

ABOUT THE AUTHOR

Alabama native Paula Graves wrote her first book, a mystery starring herself and her neighborhood friends, at the age of six. A voracious reader, Paula loves books that pair tantalizing mystery with compelling romance. When she's not reading or writing, she works as a creative director for a Birmingham advertising agency and spends time with her family and friends. She is a member of Southern Magic Romance Writers, Heart of Dixie Romance Writers and Romance Writers of America.

Paula invites readers to visit her website, www.paulagraves.com.

Books by Paula Graves

HARLEQUIN INTRIGUE

*Cooper Justice
**Cooper Justice: Cold Case Investigation
‡Cooper Security

CAST OF CHARACTERS

Evie Marsh—Cooper Security's junior accountant thinks she's over the secret crush she had on her boss. But when she's the target of a deadly group of guns-for-hire, and Jesse Cooper deems himself her personal bodyguard, will her resolve be put to the test?

Jesse Cooper—The former marine has dedicated all the resources of Cooper Security to bringing down a conspiracy that threatens countries around the globe. But when Evie Marsh becomes a target, will he risk her life to find the answers he seeks?

The Espera Group—The oil policy group has been pushing for nations across the globe to sign the Wolfsburg Treaty creating a multinational agency to control oil production and profits. But to what lengths will they go to get what they want?

Special Services Unit (SSU)—The ruthless mercenaries are paid well to thwart the Espera Group's enemies. They'll stop at nothing to use Evie Marsh against her father, a man whose secrets are putting his whole family at risk.

General Baxter Marsh—The retired Marine Corps general was one of three generals who uncovered a global conspiracy to manipulate the price and production of oil. So why is he determined to keep his secrets?

General Edward Ross—The late army general kept a coded journal during his last few years of service. But he died without revealing his part of a three-layered code key that could unlock the journal's secrets.

Rita Marsh Kingsley—Evie's older sister was once engaged to Jesse Cooper. Though recently married, does she still hold the former marine's heart?

Nolan Cavanaugh—The computer genius knows more than he's telling—and now he's in danger. Can Evie and Jesse find him before the SSU does?

Chapter One

"Have you seen Rita?"

Jesse Cooper peered through the binoculars and wondered if he could avoid answering his sister's question. He could pretend he hadn't heard her or fake a reason to get off the phone. But she'd just ask again.

He lowered the binoculars and leaned against the headrest. "Briefly." He'd spotted Rita Marsh and her mother entering Millwood Presbyterian Church a half hour earlier. Her father, General Baxter Marsh, had arrived a few minutes later alone. No idea where Evie was.

"She didn't see you, did she?"

"No." He hadn't been invited to the wedding.

"You sure we should hang back so far?" Isabel's voice held a hint of doubt. She hadn't been the only one of his brothers and sisters to question whether Jesse's "go it alone" decision had been the right one.

Jesse wasn't sure he was right either, but he couldn't pretend he wasn't worried. And because

Rita's father had hired his own security for the wedding, Jesse and his Cooper Security agents couldn't exactly form a perimeter around the church without drawing notice.

"We have to play it this way," he said. "I'll call if anything starts to go down." He said goodbye to his sister and lifted the binoculars again, focusing on a compact car swinging into a parking spot near the side of the church.

Ah, there she is.

He adjusted the lenses to watch Evie Marsh stride toward the side door of the church, muscles flexing beneath her slim-fitting jeans. A long black garment bag draped over her shoulder no doubt held her bridesmaid's dress. Jesse idly wondered what she'd look like in that dress.

Maybe he'd catch a glimpse after the wedding, when the bride and groom emerged for the rice throwing. At least he hoped it would be his first chance to see Evie in her dress—it would mean the wedding had proceeded as planned. No matter what his family thought, he'd love to see Rita Marsh married to her nice professor without incident. What he and Rita had shared had been over a long time ago.

His cell phone rang. He smiled at the name on the display. "Hi, Evie."

"Where are you positioned?"

Not much got past Rita's brainy little sister. "In

the side lot of the convenience store across the street from the church."

"How many agents with you?"

"Just me. I have others ready to move on my order."

There was a faint rustling sound on the other end of the line. Jesse's mind wandered into dangerous territory, imagining Evie undressing to put on the bridesmaid dress. He dragged his thoughts back under rigid control as she said, "I told you Dad hired a whole security team for the wedding."

"That's why I'm across the street." He checked his watch. Eleven-thirty. The wedding was at two. Attendees would be arriving soon, making it that much harder to keep an eye out for anything strange.

"I should have asked you as my date," Evie muttered.

"I don't think Rita would have appreciated that." Their relationship might be over, but he wasn't exactly one of his ex-fiancée's favorite people. "Or your dad."

"It's just stupid you're sitting over there instead of here where you can see what's going on."

"I'm hoping nothing happens and all this worry was for nothing."

"But you don't really think that's true, do you?" Evie asked. Jesse could tell she wanted to hope for the best, but she had never been a cockeyed optimist. Little Evie Marsh had always been a realist, even as a gangly teenager following Jesse and Rita around during their courtship.

"It's best to prepare for any eventuality," he answered.

He heard Evie's soft sigh over the phone. "I'd better check on Mom and Rita. I don't know who's more high-strung today."

"Is she really happy?" he asked before he could stop himself.

There was a long pause on Evie's end of the line. "Yes, she's really happy. She loves Andrew a lot."

Jesse waited for a familiar twinge of pain, but it never came. "Good," he said, meaning it.

"I'll check in again before the ceremony," she said and hung up.

Jesse closed his phone and picked up his binoculars, scanning the area for trouble and praying he'd find none.

EVIE LAID HER PHONE on the dressing table and eyed the closed door of the bride's room's inner dressing room. Rita was in there, talking with their mother as they finished the last touches on her hair and makeup. Evie wondered if her mother was asking the same question of Rita that Jesse had just asked of her.

Was she really happy?

There'd been a time Rita would have answered no. She'd spent a lot of time mourning her breakup with Jesse Cooper, although she'd been the one to end things when Jesse wouldn't give up his Marine Corps career for her.

Rita shouldn't have tried to force Jesse to be something he wasn't. He was a leatherneck through and through, even now, years after leaving the Marine Corps. It was written all over him, from his masculine bearing to his hard-toned body and high-and-tight haircut. It had never made sense to Evie that the same qualities Rita had found so irresistible were the very qualities she'd wanted him to change to be her husband.

She supposed everything worked for the best. Rita had found a man who adored her and treated her like a queen. A woman could do a lot worse than Andrew Kingsley.

Evie eyed her bridesmaid dress. She didn't relish the idea of squeezing herself into the tight bodice until absolutely necessary, but she didn't want to mess up her hair again by re-dressing in her T-shirt and jeans just to go take a look at the sanctuary. The florist had delivered the flowers earlier that morning, so she hadn't been able to get a look at the final decorations during the rehearsal the night before. She knew from her sister's description that the sanctuary was going to be beautiful. She just wanted to see it for herself.

She compromised by slipping Rita's white silk bathrobe over her slip before she padded barefoot into the corridor.

The sanctuary was at the far end of the hall, accessible by a double door that opened into the auditorium next to the piano by the altar. Evie stuck her head inside and took a quick look around.

Rita had selected an autumn palette for her wedding, her flower arrangements consisting of gold, russet and burnt-orange roses, lilies and chrysanthemums. The bridesmaid dresses were a rusty red that reminded Evie of dogwood trees in autumn. The pews were adorned with simple copper bows and the unlit unity candles at the front were a soft peach.

"Pretty, isn't it?"

Evie turned to find a man in a black tux watching her from the front pew. On the pew beside him sat a large black trumpet case.

"Beautiful," she agreed.

"I'm a little early. Or the rest of the orchestra is late." He shrugged.

He was nice-looking. Early thirties, pleasant features, trim and masculine. Also friendly and uncomplicated. She'd had about all she could take of complicated, she thought, her mind wandering to the oh-so-complicated man watching for trouble from a convenience-store parking lot.

"You're in the wedding?" the musician asked.

"Sister of the bride." She smiled. "Guess I'd better go get dressed."

She backed out of the sanctuary and started down the hall toward the bride's room. She'd gone about ten feet when she saw a rush of movement through the windows facing the church's side parking lot.

Security guards, she recognized, though the men her father had hired were in plain clothes rather than uniforms. They shared a fierceness of purpose as they streamed toward the door at the end of the corridor.

Panic tightened Evie's gut. Had something happened?

As she started sprinting toward the bride's room, someone grabbed her from behind in a strong, rough grip. She tried to struggle free, but her captor sprayed her in the face with something that stung on contact.

Pepper spray, she realized with shock, gagging as she tried to breathe. Her eyes slammed shut, burning as if on fire, and when she tried to scream, her voice came out in a tortured croak. She tried to remember the evasion methods she'd learned during her Cooper Security orientation training, but the pain in her eyes and her lungs overwhelmed her so that it was all she could do to draw her next breath.

A second captor grabbed her feet and lifted, turning her sideways and sending the world around her spinning off its axis. Blinded, gasping for air and disoriented, she landed on something solid and clawed for a foothold before realizing she was lying on her side rather than standing. She heard a solid thud of something closing, and what little light had been able to seep through her streaming eyes disappeared, plunging her into utter darkness.

The smell of pepper spray remained strong, and the skin around her face burned. She needed water, something to rinse off the residue of the spray remaining on her skin and around her eyes, but when she tried to move, she found herself confined.

She was in some sort of box. Feeling around the tiny confines of her cage, she felt the nubby texture of hard vinyl—like a case, similar to the trumpet case that had sat on the pew next to the musician in the sanctuary. But she was too large to fit into any sort of musical-instrument case. It had to be something else.

A sudden shift of position sent her sliding upside down. She put out her hands to keep her head from hitting the side of the box.

She was being moved.

A SUDDEN RUSH OF MOVEMENT across the church parking lot caught Jesse's eye. He focused his binoculars on several men racing toward the side entrance.

He dialed Evie's number. It rang three times before someone answered. "Hello?"

Not Evie, he realized with dismay. "Rita?"

There was a long pause. "Jesse?"

"I was calling Evie."

"She's not in here."

Damn. He needed to know what was going on, but he could hardly ask Rita. She'd know he was there watching the church, which would make him look like a stalker. He compromised. "Is something wrong?"

"I don't know." Rita sounded unexpectedly vulnerable. "I'm in the bloody bride's room at the church, trying to prepare for the most important day of my life, and there's an intruder supposedly prowling around the church. Now the bodyguards Daddy hired to cover the wedding have converged on the room, and I don't even have my hair done yet. The wedding is only two hours away."

Jesse frowned. An intruder?

He picked up his binoculars and scanned the area, looking for the unexpected. A few more people had arrived while he watched, bridesmaids and groomsmen either dressed for the wedding already or carrying their clothes. Parked near the sanctuary was a white panel truck with a black logo that read Audiovisual Assets—someone filming the wedding? Probably.

As he was about to look away from the truck, a couple of men came out of a side entrance carrying a large black, hard case. Frowning, he focused the binoculars on the case, which was large enough to hold a couple of oversize audio speakers. But that made no sense. Why would they be returning the speakers to the truck when the wedding hadn't happened yet?

Increasing the zoom as the men shoved the case into the truck, he spotted a scrap of white silk peeking through the narrow space between the case and its hinged cover. His internal radar pinged loudly.

"Jesse?" Rita's voice buzzed in his ear.

"What was Evie wearing the last time you saw her?" he asked.

"A slip, I think. Her dress is still hanging in here on a hook." Rita paused. "My robe is missing—she may have borrowed it to go take a look at the sanctuary. She said she wanted to take a peek before the ceremony."

That scrap of silk he saw might have been from a robe, Jesse realized, alarms sounding like a Klaxon in his brain. "I've got to go. If you see Evie, have her call me." He hung up the phone and started the car, pulling out of the parking slot and easing to the edge of the road.

The truck was on the move as well, rolling slowly toward the exit drive of the church parking lot. It paused to let passing traffic go by, then pulled onto the road, crossing in front of Jesse.

He looked at the driver. Didn't recognize him, but there was something about the man that rang all of Jesse's warning bells.

He looked like a mercenary, he realized. Military haircut, hardened expression, cold, focused eyes. There was a second man in the passenger seat of the truck cab, although Jesse didn't get a good look at him.

He pulled out his phone and called Isabel. "I'm on the move." He explained his hunch tersely. "Rita said someone tipped off the guards. It could be a decoy."

"And you think someone's kidnapped Evie?"

"I hope to hell not." He wanted to believe that any second now Evie would call him on the phone and make him feel like an idiot. A relieved idiot. But he couldn't risk staying put. "I need you to cover the church until I get back."

"Do you want anyone else to back you up?"

"No time for that. Just cover the church in case I'm wrong."

"On my way," Isabel said.

Jesse pulled onto the road, keeping a careful distance from the truck. If the driver and his comrade were indeed mercenaries, they'd know how to spot a tail. So he had to be better at tailing than they were at spotting.

He glanced at his cell phone, willing it to ring. He'd love nothing more than to be wrong about his hunch.

But the phone remained stubbornly silent.

THE RUSH OF SECURITY toward the bride's room must have been part of a diversion, Evie thought, pushing hard against the confines of her makeshift coffin. Her eyes still burned, and she was breathing with a distinct wheeze, but enough of the pain had subsided for her to shove it aside and concentrate on the bigger problem.

The box was almost as wide as it was long, which

made moving around inside easier than it might have been, but it wasn't quite long enough for her to straighten out completely. If she had to stay in this position much longer, her limbs would start to cramp up.

The sensation of movement and the engine noise rumbling in her ears confirmed she was on the move. Probably in the back of a truck. So her kidnappers didn't want her dead.

At least, not yet.

SSU, she thought. *Has to be SSU.* Since joining Cooper Security a few months earlier, she'd learned a lot about the former Special Services Unit of MacLear Security. For over a year, Jesse and the rest of the Coopers had been involved in several run-ins with the ruthless group of guns for hire who'd survived to reunite after MacLear had collapsed under the weight of scandal. Evie wasn't sure what they called themselves now, but thanks to the Coopers, she did know their activities were funded by a limited-liability company called AfterAssets.

And she knew they were after her father's secrets. They must be planning to use her as leverage against her father.

Oh, Jesse, she thought. *You were right. They did crash the wedding.*

She had to find a way out. But from the inside of a box, there wasn't a lot she could do to free herself. The borrowed robe confined her movements, especially with a piece of the hem stuck between the hinged pieces of the case. She tried tugging it free but it was firmly wedged, so she wriggled out of the robe, giving herself more mobility.

Think, Evie. What does the box look like on the outside?

It had to have latches, didn't it? She could see almost nothing inside the closed box, but by running her hands along the walls of the box, she discovered what felt like the inner workings of hinge hardware on one side, which meant there were probably latches on the other side. If she could find something to slide between the body of the box and the lid, she might be able to nudge the hasps open.

Panicked laughter bubbled in her throat. If only she'd followed Megan Cooper's suggestion to keep a knife in her bra at all times! But she wasn't a Cooper, and cloak-and-dagger shenanigans didn't come naturally to her. She had been a Cooper Security employee for just four months now, barely long enough to get through her orientation training and learn the ropes of working for a high-octane security company.

She made herself focus. No knife in her bra, but did she have something else she could use to slide through the narrow slit between the box and the lid? Maybe her earrings? They were made of copper, long and dangly, but flat and thin as well, as thin as the blade of a knife. She wasn't sure they were substantial enough to give her the leverage she needed, but it was worth a shot, wasn't it?

She took off one of her earrings, found the narrow crack between the lid and the box, and slid the copper bangle carefully into the space, moving it along until it hit resistance. Repositioning the earring, she pushed and felt something give.

Excitement bubbling in her chest, she pushed on the top of the box, testing its give. Was it her imagination or did it actually shift upward?

She wriggled down the box, probing with the earring until she met another point of resistance around the middle of the box. She repeated her earlier action, cursing when the copper earring snapped into two pieces, one remaining in her hand while the other slid through the crack and disappeared.

Sending up a prayer, she pulled the other earring from her ear and slipped it through the crack. This time, the obstruction gave way. She tested the box again. Definitely more give—through the blurry tears still burning her eyes, she saw gloomy half-light filter through the widening crack.

She had to completely shift positions to get to the final latch, wriggling until her head ended up where her feet had been. After a brief pause to catch her breath, she took care as she probed the third latch, acutely aware that if the earring broke this time, she was out of tools. The copper earring found the obstruction and she pushed against it cautiously. It gave, finally, and she laid her head back, shaking from nerves and the burning pain of pepper spray still stinging her eyes and skin.

If she'd indeed opened the final latch, the top of the box should swing open fully. All she had to do was make it happen.

Her heart pounding like a timpani in her ears, she reached up and gave the top of the box a sharp push. It opened more quickly than she anticipated, the lid swinging back and banging hard against the floor of the truck.

She froze in place, wondering if her captors had heard the noise. But the engine sound didn't change. They were still moving.

She sat up slowly, peering through the film of tears streaming from her eyes. She could make out just enough to see that the interior of the truck was nearly as dark as the interior of the box had been. With shaking hands, she pushed herself up to her feet, alarmed by the violent trembling in her legs. The truck hit a bump and she fell out of the box, landing so hard on her side that she couldn't breathe for a few seconds.

Finally able to suck air into her burning lungs, she pushed herself to her hands and knees and crawled around the truck, trying to get an idea of how large her moving prison was. She seemed to be in a vehicle about the size of a small moving truck—large enough to haul furniture or other large items but considerably smaller than a big rig. At the back was a pair of double doors, the narrow space between them delineated by a faint strip of light.

On the right side of the truck, there was the outline of another door.

She felt along the flat surface of the door, her heart sinking. There was no handle on this side of the door. She checked the other door and found no handle there either. And even if there had been, she realized, her captors would have firmly latched the door on the outside to keep her from escaping.

There was no way out.

Chapter Two

About a hundred yards ahead, the Audiovisual Assets truck pulled off the road into a gas station and parked in front of one of the pumps. In his ear, Jesse heard Evie's cell phone ring once before a deep voice came on the line. "Cooper?"

Great. Evie's father, General Baxter Marsh. Not one of Jesse's biggest fans. "Yes, sir. I was hoping Evie had turned up." He slowed near the gas station, watching the truck's driver and passenger disembark from the cab and walk into the food mart. Jesse parked on the other side of the gas pump.

"No sign of her." Marsh sounded worried. "What's going on, Cooper?"

"I told you the wedding was targeted."

"I hired security."

"Sir, I have to go. I'll call back." He hung up, aware his abrupt goodbye would hardly endear him to the general, and stepped out of the car. The truck blocked his view of the food mart, which meant it also hid him from view of anyone inside.

This might be his only chance to look inside that truck.

He eyed the cab, making sure there wasn't anyone else inside before he shifted his attention to the trailer part of the truck. On the passenger side facing him was a door set into the side of the trailer box. No padlock, just a sliding latch with a metal screw threaded through the latch to prevent it from being opened from the inside.

Interesting.

He pulled his SIG SAUER P220 from his hip holster and darted a quick look around the cab of the truck, trying to catch a glimpse of the truck's passengers inside the store. But the plate-glass windows were a mirror, bouncing his own reflection back at him. He scooted behind the cover of the truck again and took a deep breath as he eased the screw from the latch.

He swung the door open, wincing as it made a creaking noise. He listened for sound from inside, but anything he might have heard was masked by the traffic noise behind him. He was going to have to risk taking a look. Edging closer, he stuck his head inside the truck.

Out of the darkness, a foot slammed against his forehead, knocking him backward into the gas pump. As he struggled to keep his feet, a small, half-naked figure leaped from the truck and tried to dart away.

He caught a slender bare arm and held his assailant in place, despite her fierce struggle. She was small, curvy and deliciously hot, and for a second, all sensible thought leaked out of his head as his body reacted to finding her soft body pressed so intimately to his.

The flailing, red-faced creature was Evie Marsh. Her eyes were swollen nearly shut, but that didn't keep her from pounding him with her fists and feet as she tried to escape his grasp.

He shook her. "Evie, it's Jesse."

She froze, her body flattening against his, sending his head reeling again. "Jesse?" Her voice was a painful rasp.

He stared at her streaming eyes and dragged his mind out of his jeans. "What did they do to you?"

"Pepper spray," she growled. "Get me out of here now!"

He darted another quick look around the cab of the truck. The door to the food mart was open, the two men from the truck emerging with large cups of coffee. The driver locked eyes with Jesse and went instantly on alert.

"Go!" Jesse half carried Evie across the gas-pump island to his car and shoved her into the passenger seat. Driven by the sound of pounding footsteps racing across the gas station lot toward him, he slid across the hood and half dived behind the steering wheel.

So much for a clean getaway.

He jammed the key into the ignition, bracing

himself for gunshots that didn't come. Leaving the gas station in a hurry, he turned in front of an oncoming car, barely escaping a collision in a flurry of squealing brakes and a few choice gestures from the other driver.

In the rearview mirror, he spotted the truck fifty yards back, barreling toward them. He slammed the accelerator to the floor.

"Are they behind us?" Evie turned in the passenger seat, squinting.

"No way can that truck catch us." The extra weight of the truck would give Jesse the advantage, but if he didn't keep other vehicles between him and the truck, a high-powered rifle could quickly even the playing field.

He also had the advantage of knowing the back roads of Chickasaw County better than their pursuers, whipping the Ford Taurus down a pothole-pocked blacktop road. The road cut past Mill Pond, where he'd caught one of the biggest bluegills he'd ever seen, and twisted up the southern face of Gossamer Mountain. Over the hill lay Gossamer Lake and home.

He checked the rearview mirror frequently. No sign of the truck.

"Do you have any water?" Evie tried to stifle a cough.

Jesse reached into the backseat to retrieve the bag of supplies he'd packed for his stakeout. He handed Evie a bottle of water from the bag, and she flushed her face and eyes. "Someone grabbed me at the church. Sprayed me right in the face with pepper spray. I couldn't even catch my breath long enough to yell for help."

"How about now? You breathing okay?"

"Mostly." She coughed again. "I'm better."

He pulled out his phone and dialed his brother Rick's cell number.

Rick answered on the first ring. "Where are you?"

Jesse caught his brother up on what had happened. "I've got Evie, but I'm not sure I should take her back to the church. Can you call Evie's cell number? Someone will answer and you can tell them Evie's safe."

"I'm not ruining Rita's wedding!" Evie protested.

Jesse slanted a quick look at her. "That can't be a consideration, Evie. You know that."

"Am I your prisoner?" she shot back, her glare lethal even through swollen eyelids.

"You think putting yourself and the rest of your family at greater risk is going to make her happier?" Jesse argued.

"Take me back to the church, Jesse."

"Take her to the church," Rick said. "We'll meet you there."

Jesse pressed his lips into a thin line, every instinct telling him to stash Evie in the nearest safe house. But was he letting his affection for Rita's kid sister get in the way of his good sense? He needed

Baxter Marsh's cooperation now more than ever. Spiriting his daughter away without even consulting him was hardly going to win him over.

"Okay," he said aloud, ignoring the twisting sensation in his gut. "We'll go back to the church."

"You can't postpone the wedding." Evie looked at her sister in dismay. "All that money going to waste? It's ridiculous."

Rita's lips curved in a faint smile. "Trust you to look at it from an accounting perspective."

"Rita, please. If you postpone it now, we let those creeps win."

"You can't walk down the aisle when you can barely see, Evie." Rita winced as she looked at Evie's face. "And I know you were looking forward to being my maid of honor."

"I was looking forward to your getting married to a man who makes you happy," Evie answered, even though her sister was right. She *had* been looking forward to being her sister's maid of honor.

Their relationship over the years hadn't always been close, especially during the teenage years when Rita had resented her younger sister's constant tagging along, and Evie had been jealous of Rita's being first to do everything. But they'd forged a strong bond over the past few years, and being her sister's chosen attendant had been a big deal to Evie.

"Oh, Evie," Rita murmured, her eyes filling with tears.

"I want you to marry Andrew and be disgustingly happy for the rest of your life. That's all that matters."

Rita's gaze slanted to her left, where Jesse Cooper stood near the wall of the bride's room, a silent sentinel. Evie wondered what her sister was thinking about her ex's presence. She had tried to warn Jesse that coming into the bride's room with her might not be the best idea, but he'd refused to let her out of his sight. Apparently he'd assigned himself to be her personal bodyguard, and he took the job very seriously.

"I should thank him," Rita said, reluctance thick in her voice.

"It's not necessary. He lives for this kind of thing."

Rita's lips curled upward again. "I know."

Evie supposed she did. Jesse Cooper hadn't changed much in the past ten years, despite his change of careers. The same strong sense of honor, duty and ethics he'd learned in the Marine Corps had traveled with him to his new job as head of Cooper Security.

"I'm glad he came." Rita kept her voice low so that it wouldn't carry to where Jesse stood watch. Evie suspected it was a futile effort; knowing Jesse, he could probably read lips.

"Why's that?" she asked Rita.

"Because it helped me be absolutely sure I'm over him."

"You didn't know that before you said yes to Andrew?" Evie tried to arch an eyebrow, but the stinging pain of her swollen eyes wouldn't allow it.

"I thought I knew. I was pretty sure I knew." Rita smiled. "But now I know for certain."

Evie darted a quick look at Jesse, wondering if he was over Rita, as well. Their courtship had been intense and passionate, their breakup equally explosive. Even now, Jesse couldn't hide his reaction whenever Rita's name came up in conversation.

"Are you sure, Evie? About our going ahead with the wedding?"

"Positive," she answered. "And who knows? I have an hour to recover. If I'm feeling better, I can put a little extra makeup on to cover the redness and swelling. Besides, everyone will be looking at you anyway."

Rita took a deep breath before she spoke. "Okay, then. We'll go ahead with the wedding. Try putting cold compresses on your eyes. I want you up there with me." She gave Evie a quick, fierce hug.

As Rita followed their mother back to the private chamber to finish her preparations for the wedding, Evie dropped wearily on the nearby bench, pressing her hands to her throbbing forehead. The stinging burn of the pepper spray had mostly subsided, and her vision had cleared up considerably, but those irritations had been replaced by the beginning of a brain-pounding headache. She hoped it would ease off soon because she was going to do everything she could to stand at the altar as her sister's maid of honor, headache or not.

"You okay?"

She looked up at Jesse's gravel-voiced query. "Yeah. Just working on a headache. All the stress, I guess."

Evie's father crossed to her side, subtly positioning himself between her and Jesse. "Do you need ibuprofen?"

"That would be great."

Her father pulled a small pillbox from his pocket and fished out a couple of pain relievers. He slanted a pointed look at Jesse. "There's a water fountain in the hall with a paper-cup dispenser."

Jesse frowned, clearly not happy about leaving Evie alone, even with her father, but he'd been a Marine long enough to balk at disobeying an order from a general. He disappeared through the door.

"We need to call the police," her father said. "They should be looking for the truck."

"Jesse thinks the local police aren't equipped to handle the men who kidnapped me."

"Jesse thinks." Her father grimaced. "Jesse thinks a lot of things."

"He's right about this. You know he is."

"He thinks the men who took you were SSU agents." There was little skepticism in her father's voice, despite his obvious dislike for Jesse. He knew as well as anyone just how ruthless the mercenaries who'd once worked for MacLear Security could be. One of his most trusted colleagues had already died at their hands, and another had spent nearly a month as a captive of the deadly soldiers of fortune, along with his wife and daughter.

"I'm pretty sure Jesse's right about that, too."

Her father touched her face, his fingers gentle. "You're not keeping anything from me, are you? They didn't hurt you more than you've said—"

"No, they didn't. But given time, they would have."

Her father met her gaze for a long, electric moment, then looked away.

"You need to talk to Jesse about General Ross's journal."

Her father's mouth tightened but he didn't answer.

Evie gave a little growl of frustration. "I don't know why you're being so stubborn about this, Dad. Look what happened today—you think they won't go after us again? Maybe Rita this time, or Mom. And Jesse Cooper won't be there to save them."

His gaze snapped up to meet hers, pain vibrating in his blue eyes. "I'm doing what I can to protect us all."

"By staying silent? That's not enough for these people. You have to know it's not. I don't understand why you don't just tell people what you do know, even if you don't have proof."

"I'll increase our security team," her father said, ignoring her last comment.

"Are you going to make them aware of the level of the threat against us?" She shook her head. "If you put the average security guard up against the SSU, he'll lose every time."

She knew her father couldn't argue. He'd been around for the downfall of MacLear Security, a once well-respected private security firm that had done business with the Pentagon for years. MacLear Security's training corps had been made up of top-notch former military and law-enforcement personnel. Even the company's legitimate agents had possessed the knowledge and skills of elite soldiers. And the Special Services Unit, MacLear's secret unit of guns for hire, had layered those skills in with an utter lack of a moral compass.

Ruthless and violent, the SSU had been a wickedly efficient private army for a corrupt State Department official named Barton Reid. Their work for Reid had eventually led to the company's downfall, thanks to Jesse's cousins, who'd thwarted the secret soldiers' plans to abduct a child as leverage. The Coopers had exposed MacLear's seamy underbelly and brought the company down, but not before several of the SSU operatives had made their escape and formed a new alliance.

Funded by a mysterious company called After-Assets, LLC, the dirty operatives had recently been involved in at least one assassination and another assassination attempt. They'd kidnapped an Air Force general and his family and now had tried to kidnap Evie, as well.

"They want General Ross's journal," she said.

"Do you know where it is?" her father asked.

She shook her head. "But they think you do."

"I don't know where it went after Cooper took it from Lydia Ross," the general murmured, glancing toward the door. "I bet he knows."

"Probably so. But it's important nobody else knows where it is, because you seem determined not to tell us what you know."

He bent toward her, as if he was going to tell her something, but a soft knock on the door interrupted. Evie crossed to the door. "Yes?"

"It's me," Jesse said from the other side of the door.

She let him in. He slipped inside, handing her a cup of water.

"Thanks." She downed the two ibuprofen tablets her father had given her. "That took longer than I thought—did you get a call? Any news?"

He glanced at her father briefly, then looked back at her. "Rick and Megan found the truck abandoned on the side of the road two miles up from the gas station where I found you. We're processing it for prints, but it's not likely we'll find anything."

"You should bring the real police into this," Evie's father said with a grimace. "You're screwing up any chance of a court case against these guys."

"A court isn't going to stop these guys. Half of them were already indicted along with Barton Reid, and you see how well that stopped them," Evie told her father. "The bigger picture is what matters. We need to stop whoever's funneling money to them to pull these jobs."

"I know you think the Espera Group may have something to do with it." Jesse looked at her father. "I know you want to expose their real agenda. But to do that, you have to let me help you."

Evie winced as her father's expression grew stony. "I don't have to do anything," he snapped. "Except make sure my daughter gets married today to a fine man who treats her like a queen."

Jesse didn't flinch outwardly, but Evie didn't miss the slight flicker of anger that darkened his eyes. "Very well." He turned to Evie. "I'll wait outside until you're dressed, then I'll escort you to the chapel."

"That won't be necessary," her father said. "I've already assigned one of my security guards to stick with Evie wherever she goes today."

Jesse's eyes narrowed. "Because they did such a good job before?"

Evie put her hand on her father's arm. His muscles were hard with tension, but he remained silent as she looked at Jesse.

"I'll be okay," she said, although she wasn't sure she was right. But having Jesse around today of all days was too stressful for everyone. Despite her earlier reassurances, Rita couldn't be happy about Jesse crashing her wedding, however good his reasons.

"I'll just go back to what I was doing earlier today, then," he said.

She hid a smile. Back to the convenience-store parking lot, then. Watching over the wedding from afar.

A part of her wished she could believe his concern was specifically for her and not her family in general. Like Rita, she'd never been immune to Jesse Cooper's sexy strength and leatherneck sense of honor. But unlike Rita, Evie didn't find his hard-driving, adrenaline-soaked lifestyle a deal breaker. In fact, she craved the sort of meaning and purpose he seemed to find in risking his neck to help people. It was one reason why she'd taken him up on the offer of a job at Cooper Security.

But not the only reason.

Unfortunately, Jesse clearly saw her as Rita's little sister and nothing more. So that was that. Time to get over her schoolgirl crush on Jesse and move on.

Still, her gaze remained on the bride's room door long after he'd closed it behind him.

Chapter Three

The bride and groom emerged from the back of the church to a cheering crowd of well-wishers tossing birdseed. Jesse couldn't resist the urge to raise his binoculars for a closer look, focusing on the pink cheeks and bright eyes of the bride.

Rita was stunning. At thirty-two, she looked nearly a decade younger, her fair skin unlined. Her cornflower-blue eyes glowed with a joy he could see even through the impersonal lenses of the binoculars.

She was happy. It radiated from her like sunshine, warming him from a distance. There had been a time when he'd have resented her finding someone else who could make her happy, but those days were long gone. Maturity and experience had softened the edges of his jealous nature and time had taught him that real love was unselfish.

He would always love Rita and want the best for her, but that didn't mean he had to be the one to give it to her. If he'd been able to do that—and if she'd been able to make him happy as well—they would still be together.

Suit-clad men surrounded the bride and groom, guiding them down the sidewalk toward a limousine parked nearby. The reception would take place at The Lodge on Gossamer Lake, a sprawling resort on a scenic overlook with a stunning view of the lake. Jesse already had agents positioned there to augment General Marsh's security contingent.

He watched the limousine move with a stately lack of urgency, the bride and groom waving at their well-wishers as they passed near the front of the church on their way out.

Jesse's phone rang. Isabel. "You got the limo?"

"I'm on it," she said. "You're going to keep an eye on Evie and her parents?"

He spotted Evie waving at the passing limousine. Her face was still a little puffy and red, but her makeup job had hidden the worst of it, and her small, compact body looked amazing in the dark red gown she'd worn as her sister's maid of honor.

Sometime in the past ten years, Rita's gangly little sister had grown into a woman. She wasn't tall and willowy like Rita, but what she lacked in height, she made up in lush curves in all the right places.

She'd been working out at the Cooper Security gym; Jesse had spotted her there a few times when he'd been working out himself. She'd taken the fitness ethic of Cooper Security seriously, even though her work was confined to the accounting department, and he'd seen the results of her efforts a few weeks ago when she'd been caught in a late-night ambush at the office.

She'd held her own, despite being injured and drugged by an SSU operative who'd been part of a siege on the building. Jesse had been impressed.

So why hadn't he told her so?

Evie followed her parents to a black SUV driven by one of the security guards Jesse had seen earlier outside the bride's room. But she didn't get inside, shaking her head as her father clearly tried to coax her to join them. Finally, he stopped arguing and joined her mother in the SUV.

Frowning, Jesse watched the SUV drive away, his chest tightening with alarm. What the hell was she thinking? He sent a quick text to his brother Rick, who was parked nearby.

General and wife in black SUV. Follow.

He adjusted the binoculars and saw Evie was holding her cell phone in her hand. She punched a button and lifted the phone to her ear. A second later, Jesse's phone rang.

He didn't bother with a greeting. "Have you lost your mind?"

"Stop worrying."

"Where's your bodyguard?"

"On his way." She pointed to a lanky man approaching from her left. "I just thought it would be better if we didn't all go in the same vehicle to the reception. I keep thinking about what happened to the Harlowes."

She had a point. General Emmett Harlowe, his wife and his daughter had all been kidnapped together from the north Georgia vacation cabin they owned. Spreading the Marsh family into different vehicles would make it hard for the SSU to get to them all.

"Be careful, okay?"

"You going to join us at the lodge?" she asked, falling into step with the guard as they walked toward a navy SUV parked nearby.

"That's the plan."

"There's not a convenience store across the street where you can lurk."

He smiled at the humor in her voice. "That's okay. I know that area about as well as I know any place in the world. I'll figure out something."

"My guard is giving me the stink eye. I guess I need to get off the phone."

"Be careful."

"You, too." She sounded serious.

He hung up and lifted the binoculars again, watching until she was safely inside the SUV. He started his car and pulled up to the road, waiting for Evie and her guard to pass. He didn't bother trying to keep his distance. If the guard spotted him, Evie could explain his presence.

No way was he letting Evie out of his sight this time.

"HE'S NOT A DANGER," Evie told the guard in the driver's seat, a lanky, quiet man in his early forties. Her father had introduced him as Alan Wilson, a former Jefferson County prison guard. "He's my boss."

"Jesse Cooper?" Wilson asked.

"You've heard of him?"

"Everyone in the security business has heard of him."

She felt a surge of pride and had to remind herself that she had little right to feel flattered by any praise for Cooper Security. She'd worked there less than half a year as an accountant, and she certainly had no right to take pride in any of Jesse Cooper's accomplishments.

He was just her boss. Not even her direct boss— there were a couple of layers of middle management between them at least. And any personal connection between them had been severed completely less than an hour ago when her sister had married someone else.

She turned to look behind them, spotting Jesse's car only forty yards back. She couldn't see him through the glare on the windshield, but she took comfort knowing he was there. They started around a curve, temporarily hiding Jesse's car from view. With a sigh, Evie turned back to face front.

And gasped as she spotted two cars sprawled across the road ahead.

Wilson spat out a couple of quick profanities, slamming on the brakes. Only the seat belt and her feet planted on the floorboard kept Evie from pitching through the windshield.

The brakes shrieked, the chassis shuddered as the SUV's wheels struggled for traction, eating up a terrifying amount of the narrow distance between them and the cars ahead. Evie braced herself for a collision.

They stopped a few yards short of impact. Wilson's hands trembled on the steering wheel.

Evie pressed her hand to her pounding heart. "My God."

She looked behind them, expecting to find Jesse's car right on their bumper. But he'd stopped well short. Of course. Nothing ever seemed to catch Jesse Cooper by surprise.

A cracking sound, incredibly close, drew her attention away from the car behind her. She felt something warm and wet splash her and looked at Wilson for an explanation.

For a moment, she couldn't process what she was seeing. He was still upright, still facing forward, just as he'd been a moment before. But where his head met the headrest, blood and brain tissue splattered the upholstery.

Another cracking sound made her duck behind the dashboard. The window beside her disintegrated, pebbles of glass falling around her. In rapid succession, two more shots rang in the air.

Oh God oh God oh God!

She was still in her bridesmaid dress, shackled by the tight bodice and long skirt. Her feet tangled in the folds of satin as she unbuckled her seat belt and tried to crawl onto the floorboard to protect herself from more gunfire.

She needed a weapon. Some way to fight back.

She eyed the butt of the Smith & Wesson 9mm pistol peeking out from beneath Wilson's blood-stained jacket. Tamping down a flood of nausea, she grabbed the weapon, grappling with the holster until she'd tugged it free.

She dared a quick peek over the dashboard. The two cars remained where they were, blocking the road. She could see a couple of men crouched behind the cars, the tops of their heads barely visible. Another gunshot rang out and they disappeared from sight.

Jesse, she realized. He was giving her cover fire.

If she could get back to his car, she had a chance. He'd get her out of here, away from the ambush. He'd take her somewhere safe.

But only if she could get to him.

The dress was a liability. She couldn't run in the

long skirt and didn't have time or room to undress without putting herself in the line of fire. But if she could get rid of the skirt, she might have a chance.

She grabbed the fabric at the seam where the bodice met the skirt, took a deep breath and pulled as hard as she could. The satin tore away with a satisfying rip. She found the tear and pulled harder, separating the skirt from the bodice until it fell away completely. Wriggling free of the skirt, she grabbed the Smith & Wesson and took another peek over the dashboard just in time to see one of the assailants take another shot.

The bullet thudded against the frame of the car, shaking the whole vehicle. She swallowed a fresh flood of nausea and ducked again.

Okay, think. You've got to get back to Jesse. That means you may have to do a little shooting of your own.

She wasn't a great shot, but thanks to her recent orientation training at Cooper Security, she knew how to lay down cover fire. Of course, doing that while running was a whole other thing altogether, but what choice did she have? Wait for Jesse to run to her rescue? That would just put him in the line of fire, too. And if she didn't make her move soon, that was exactly what Jesse would do.

He wasn't the kind of guy who'd hang back and let the situation unfold.

She took a deep breath and visualized her next moves. Open the door. Use it for cover as she fired off a couple of rounds, forcing the men behind the cars to duck. Then run like hell to Jesse's car and hope she could get out of the line of fire before the ambushers got a chance to shoot back.

She tugged the door handle but nothing happened. It was locked.

She swallowed a frustrated curse and shoved the lock open. Gunfire split the air, making her flinch, but it seemed to come from behind her, so she made her move, swinging the door open.

Scrambling out, she kept her body behind the door and rose just long enough to fire a couple of shots through the shattered window. Then she whipped around and started running.

She spotted Jesse crouched behind his car door, his gun already firing a rapid fusillade of cover fire. Reaching the passenger door, she jerked it open and dived inside, hunkering on the floorboard.

Jesse fired three more rounds, already sliding behind the steering wheel. He fired a final shot as he turned the key in the ignition and slammed into Reverse.

Evie curled into a knot on the floorboard as they rocketed backward for a few endless seconds. Then the car whipped around, flinging her sideways into the door, and shot suddenly forward.

"Stay down!" Jesse barked.

She did as he asked, her pulse thundering in her ears, drowning out the roar of the car's engine and the squeal of tires as Jesse navigated the winding mountain road at breakneck speed.

After what seemed like hours, the car slowed to a normal speed, and Jesse spoke again, his voice hard and tense. "You can get in the seat now. Buckle up in case we have to make another run for it."

Slowly, she pushed herself up into the passenger seat, her leg muscles trembling as if she'd been running for miles. With shaking hands, she buckled her seat belt and stared at Jesse's set profile, her breath coming in short, harsh gasps.

"Are you okay?" he asked without looking away from the road.

"Yeah," she answered.

He slanted a quick look at her, a hint of amusement in his dark eyes as he took in her state of undress. "You're rough on clothes, Marsh."

She managed a shaky laugh that faded quickly as she saw the blood on her arms. "What do you think they'll do with Mr. Wilson's body?"

He shook his head. "I don't know. They might dispose of it to get rid of evidence."

She blinked back tears. "Damn it."

He pulled his cell phone out of his pocket and pushed a speed-dial number. "We've got trouble," he told whoever answered.

Evie laid her head against the headrest and closed her eyes, trying not to give in to a sudden assault of nausea. The last seconds of Alan Wilson's life played in her head like a skipping record, repeating the horror until she wanted to scream.

She heard the engine downshift, felt the forward motion of Jesse's car slow and opened her eyes. Jesse had pulled off the main road and headed down a narrow dirt track that seemed to lead right into the middle of the woods. He put the car in Park, killing the engine.

"Do you need to throw up?" he asked flatly.

She looked at him. "No." She swallowed hard and regained control over her rebellious stomach.

"It's okay if you do." He bent toward her, his body brushing hers as he opened the glove compartment and pulled out a small canvas bag. He handed it to her. "It's a first-aid kit, but there are some wet wipes inside. Clean up—you'll feel better."

She found the wipes and cleaned off the sticky evidence of Alan Wilson's murder. "They're fearless."

"I think the word you're looking for is *ruthless*."

"They're not afraid of the police. They're not afraid of being caught."

"They don't want to be caught. But they're willing to take chances."

She struggled with tears, hating herself for her weakness. "We have to stop those sons of bitches. Whatever it takes."

Jesse turned to face her, reaching out one big

hand to cup her chin. He made her look at him. "We will."

A horrifying thought occurred to her. "What if someone ambushed Rita or my parents?"

"Rick's following your parents. I just talked to him—they made it to the reception just fine. And Rita was already there, so she's safe, too."

"Unless they go after them at the reception."

"I'm not sure they'll want to take on that many people at once," Jesse said. "But I've already called in reinforcements to cover the perimeter. Rick's going to tell your family what's going on."

"What happens now?"

His hand lingered a moment, his fingers warm against her jawline. "We're going to a safe house."

"We?"

"You and me."

"Oh."

He cocked his head. "Is that a problem?"

She shook her head. "No. No problem."

Except it was. It was a huge problem. It was hard enough getting over her lingering feelings for her boss when she passed him in the hallway at Cooper Security three or four times a week.

How was she supposed to move on with her life stuck in a safe house with him 24/7?

THE SAFE HOUSE TURNED OUT to be a modest A-frame house on the western shore of Gossamer Lake, miles across the water from Cooper Cove Marina, the marina and fishing camp run by Jesse's uncle and cousins. "Cooper Security bought it last year through a third party so it can't be easily traced to us," Jesse had explained as he led Evie inside.

There were three bedrooms. Jesse let her pick the one she wanted. She selected one of the two corner rooms, a surprisingly large and airy room with pleasant blue walls and simple navy curtains that blocked out the afternoon sunlight, sparing her still-aching eyes.

There was a bathroom at one end of the room, well stocked with plain, soft towels, washcloths, and a selection of soaps and shampoos. She tugged off her bloodstained clothes quickly and took a long, hot shower, trying to scrub out the horrors of the afternoon.

But only the blood washed away.

In the bedroom closet, she found clothes and shoes. Looking through them, she discovered they were mostly women's clothes, in a variety of sizes ranging from petite to tall. The shoes spanned several sizes as well—apparently Cooper Security liked to cover all its bases.

She found a pair of jeans and a charcoal-gray T-shirt to replace her slip and half a bridesmaid dress. A pair of slip-on sandals replaced the rust-colored pumps that were making her feet hurt. She twisted her hair into a knot at the back of her head, anchoring it with a pencil she found on the writing desk by the bed.

She checked her reflection in the dresser mirror. She looked a wreck, her red-rimmed eyes wide and haunted.

Get control, Marsh. You can handle this.

Taking a deep, bracing breath, she wiped the shell-shocked look from her face and went back to the front room to look for Jesse.

She found him on his cell phone, talking to his brother. "Rick, tell Aaron we'll both give him a statement as soon as we feel safe, but first, he has to find the shooters. I gave you the description." Jesse looked up as she entered, his dark-eyed gaze typically inscrutable. Jesse was a cipher. Always had been, even as a young Marine recruit madly in love with a general's daughter. Evie wasn't sure Rita had realized just how complicated a man she'd fallen for, but Evie had known all along.

It was one of the most irresistible things about him. Who didn't love a mystery?

"Make sure her parents and sister know she's okay," he said into the phone. "They'll probably want to see her—"

"And I want to see them," she said firmly.

He held up one finger, annoying her. She clamped her mouth closed and sat on the sofa opposite his chair.

"Tell them it's not safe." Jesse shot her a pointed look. She pressed her lips together more tightly and held her tongue, waiting until he finished with his brother. When he finally hung up the phone, he turned to look at her, preempting her next words. "Your parents will be calling from a secure phone in about twenty minutes."

"I want to see them, not just talk to them."

"Evie, someone just tried to kidnap you a second time. We're damned lucky we're both still alive."

She knew he was right, but she didn't have to like it. "I can't imagine my father will be happy about this situation."

Jesse's eyebrow ticked upward. "I'm sure you're right."

"What are you going to tell him when he calls?"

"That you need protection."

"He'll want his own people to guard me."

Jesse's mouth set in a grim line. "Too bad."

"Don't goad him about it."

"I won't. But he's being stubborn. He's not going to find a security crew better equipped to handle the threat than Cooper Security. We know more about the SSU and AfterAssets than anyone out there. We have an entire section dedicated to bringing them down. He should let us help him protect not just you but the rest of your family, as well."

"I'm on your side, Jesse. You don't have to convince me."

"I know." His gaze shifted slightly, and she looked down to see that the T-shirt she'd selected was stretched tight across her breasts.

Self-consciously, she crossed her arms in front of her. "I could use some clothes that fit better."

"I know. Tell me your size and I'll have someone do some shopping at the thrift store in Gossamer Ridge for you." Jesse leaned closer, his gaze narrowed as he searched her face. "Your eyes still look pretty red and swollen. Do they hurt?"

"They're better." They weren't stinging anymore, although the sensitive skin around her eyes felt tender and raw. "The blurry vision has gone away."

To her surprise, he reached out and touched her cheek. "I'm so sorry about what you've been through today. I know it had to be terrifying."

"I didn't have time to think about it," she admitted. "Not then."

He dropped his hand to cover hers. His palm was warm and dry, driving home how cold her own hands were.

With a look of apology, he said, "I need you to tell me everything you can remember about the last few hours."

Chapter Four

Evie eased her hands away from Jesse's grasp and sat up straighter. "You know they grabbed me outside the sanctuary. I told you that, right?"

He nodded. "They put you in that box I saw them carrying."

"Right. I think it was one of those big cases large audio speakers go in."

Jesse nodded. "That makes sense. The truck had a logo on the side—Audiovisual Assets."

"Assets." The word clicked into focus. "As in AfterAssets?"

He looked surprised. "I hadn't thought about that. But because we're pretty sure those guys were former SSU operatives, it makes sense."

"They definitely gave off the stench of the SSU. All business. I was out of commission and stuck in that box before I had time to think."

"How did you get out?"

She managed a grin. "I used my earrings to slide

through the space between the box and the lid to push the latches open."

He smiled. "Everybody always underestimates you, don't they?"

She felt ridiculously pleased at the indirect compliment. "At their peril," she said with a bright bravado she didn't quite feel. The full impact of what had happened to her had begun to sink in. Jesse was right—she'd been lucky today. Twice. "How did you know to follow the truck anyway?"

"A hunch," he admitted. He told her about seeing the silk sticking out of the box. "When I called your phone and got Rita, I couldn't shake the feeling that you were inside that box."

She tamped down a shiver. "Thank God for your hunches."

He got up from his chair and sat beside her on the sofa, sliding his arm around her shoulder. She fought the urge to sink into his arms, acutely aware of the danger that lay behind that desire.

Beyond the fact that he was her boss, he was also about as off-limits as a man came. He'd been her sister's fiancé, and she was pretty sure he still harbored feelings for Rita that would never go away. She'd already spent her whole life coming in second to her brilliant, beautiful sister. She wasn't going to do that with Jesse Cooper. It was long past time to let go of her girlhood crush on him.

Jesse's cell phone rang, giving her an excuse

to ease out of his grasp. He looked at the display, frowning a little as he answered. "Hello?"

After a pause, he held out the phone to her. "Your father."

She took the phone, dismayed at how her hand was shaking. "Daddy?"

Her father's deep growl rumbled over the phone line. "Kitten, are you okay? Cooper's brother told me what happened to you."

"I'm fine." She blinked back the unexpected tears stinging her eyes. It had been a long time since her father had used his old pet name for her. Their relationship had been difficult for the past few months, ever since she'd told him she was taking the accounting job at Cooper Security. It was good to hear him speak to her without the strain of disapproval.

"You don't sound fine. What happened exactly?"

She told her father about the ambush, trying to make it sound less scary than it had been at the time. "Jesse helped me get away. I was lucky."

"You tell Cooper you want to come home."

"Daddy—"

"I'll hire extra security."

"Hire Cooper Security," she said. "We're all still in danger. And the security team you've hired isn't capable of dealing with these people."

"You think I can't protect you?"

"I know you'd do everything you could. But this is big, Dad. You know that better than any of us."

He was silent a moment.

"Daddy, please talk to Jesse. Tell him everything you know about the Espera Group. Give him your part of the code to the journal."

"Evie, none of this concerns you."

"It all concerns me. They're trying to use us against you because of what you know."

"And flapping my jaws about what I know will only make things that much worse. I'm trying to protect you girls and your mama."

"It's not working."

"I know what I'm doing."

She bit back a retort she knew would only hurt her father. "I do, too. Jesse and the Coopers know what we're up against. I trust them to protect me. And maybe it's smarter if we're not all together in one place."

"I don't agree."

"I know. I'm sorry."

There was a long silence on the phone line between them. She broke it a moment later by asking, "How's Mom? How are Rita and Andrew?"

"Rita and Andrew just left for the hotel."

Rita and her new husband were flying to Spain for their honeymoon the next morning, but they'd made plans to spend the night at a hotel in Birmingham. "You should hire Cooper Security to provide them with protection. Spain isn't unreachable. And the hotel is probably vulnerable."

"I'm taking care of it," her father said flatly. "Your mother wants to talk to you."

After a brief pause, her mother came on the line, her voice tight with tears. "Baby girl, are you sure you're okay?"

"I'm fine," she assured her. "Really."

"I can't believe all of this is happening." Her mother's voice was dark with dismay. "First Edward Ross, then what happened to the Harlowes and now all this—"

"We're going to figure it all out," Evie said firmly.

"Here's your father again."

Her father came back on the line. "Let me speak to Cooper."

Evie held out the phone to Jesse. "He wants to speak to you."

Jesse took the phone, looking unperturbed. "General." He listened a moment, glancing at Evie. "I can't do that, sir." He hung up the phone.

"Did you hang up on him?"

"He ordered me to take you home to him."

She arched her eyebrows. "Ordered you?"

"He's worried about you. And probably feeling guilty about the danger you're in." Jesse shot her a considering look. "He *should* feel guilty. I know he's trying to protect you all, but he's going about it the wrong way. I wish he'd let us provide protection for your family."

"He's never going to do that. It would be like admitting he was wrong about you, and you know how he hates to admit he's wrong." As Jesse started to move toward the sofa where she sat, she pushed to her feet, putting distance between them. She felt vulnerable and needy at the moment, and letting Jesse Cooper anywhere near her when she was in that condition was asking for a disaster. "I think I'd like to lie down awhile. You probably have more calls to make, right?"

His dark eyes narrowed as if he were seeing right past her excuses to discern the motives behind them. She crossed her arms in front of her, feeling suddenly naked.

"Okay," he said. "Call me if you need me."

"Will do," she said over her shoulder as she retreated to the bedroom.

But she wouldn't call him. Because the last thing she ever intended to do again was need Jesse Cooper.

THE SAFE HOUSE was eerily silent, offering no distraction from the maelstrom of images racing through Jesse's mind. He was a twelve-year veteran of the U.S. Marine Corps, had seen combat on three different continents and had killed more than one enemy soldier during his time in uniform. He'd made peace with what he'd been called upon to do by remembering his sacred duty to protect not only his countrymen at home but his brothers-in-arms fighting in the trenches with him.

So why couldn't he get the chaotic sounds and images of the recent ambush out of his head?

Because it was Evie Marsh they'd been gunning for.

Jesse rubbed his jaw, his mind fixed on the sight

of her pushing open the door of the dead security guard's SUV and racing through the hail of bullets to reach Jesse's position. Her blue eyes had been wide and scared, but she'd run without hesitation, trusting him to lay down cover fire to get her safely out of harm's way.

As vulnerable as she'd looked, barely clad in the ruins of her rust-colored dress with her fancy hairdo falling around her face in a messy cloud, her courage had been a sucker punch right to his gut.

Hearing a door open in the back of the house, his hand went automatically to the pistol holstered at his hip. He relaxed when, a moment later, Evie emerged from the hallway looking soft and sleepy-eyed.

"What time is it?" she asked.

He glanced at his watch. "Around nine forty-five. You slept awhile. You hungry? Not much here except canned stuff, but I could heat up some soup or something." He'd had soup and crackers for his own dinner.

She shook her head and sat on the sofa beside him, her body radiating warmth. "Any news while I was playing Rip van Winkle?"

"All quiet."

She pulled her bare feet up to the sofa, tucking her knees to her chest and wrapping her arms around them. "I suppose it was too much to hope they'd nab those guys trying to leave the state."

"I doubt they've tried to leave the state."

Evie's gaze slanted up to meet his. "No, they're not exactly the type to retreat when their mission doesn't go right the first time, are they?"

"They're probably already ticked off about losing the Harlowes last month. Especially without getting the general's part of the code out of any of them. They need a win." Jesse tried to study Evie's appearance without her noticing his scrutiny. She looked tired but the swelling and redness around her eyes and nose had gone down considerably. By morning she'd have few signs of her run-in with the pepper spray.

There was a faint purple bruise on her cheekbone, however, that might look worse the next day. He brushed his fingertips against the blemish before he could stop himself. Her gaze snapped up to his.

"You have a bruise."

She backed away from his touch. "Must have banged my face on that box when they were pushing me inside."

"Are you sure that's all it was?"

"Nobody hit me. Believe me, I'd have told you." Her lips curved in a wry, humorless grin. "Though I'd take getting socked in the face three times a day over being shot at."

Something in the tone of her voice made his gut ache. "Did you have a nightmare about it? While you were asleep?"

She looked away. "I don't remember."

She did remember. Vividly. He could tell by the look on her face, the tense set of her shoulders and the white-knuckled grip of her clasped hands.

"I used to have combat-related nightmares all the time. Still do sometimes."

"So they don't go away?" Despair tinged her voice.

"They usually soften with time. Sharp edges dull, sounds mute." Blood didn't run as freely or as crimson-dark after a while.

"I don't know if Wilson had a family," she murmured after a moment of tense silence. "I don't even remember if he wore a wedding ring."

"You didn't get him killed, Evie."

"He wouldn't be dead if he hadn't been guarding me."

"He wouldn't be dead if those men hadn't shot him. That wasn't your doing." He slid his arm across the back of the sofa, letting his fingers brush against the curve of her shoulder. "First rule of engagement—remember who's the good guy and who's the bad guy."

"No, the first rule of engagement is to be courteous to everyone but friendly to no one," she countered.

He smiled. Should have known he wouldn't get that one past the daughter of a Marine Corps general. "You'd have been a good Marine."

The wistful look she gave him caught him off

guard. "I wanted to be a Marine. Did you know that?"

He shook his head, surprised. "No. Why didn't you?"

"Mother didn't want another Marine to have to worry about. And Dad agreed." She rested her cheek on her knee, still looking up at him. "I could have defied them. Hell, maybe I should have. But I couldn't put my mother through another twenty years of anxiety, especially so close to my father's retirement date."

He tried to imagine Evie in uniform. She was small but physically strong, as he'd experienced when she'd kicked him in the face earlier that day. He'd watched enough of her Cooper Security training sessions to know she was agile and skillful. She had a decent record at the shooting range, and her thinking skills were top-notch.

The only disadvantage she'd have had as a Marine was her size, and she could have made up much of that deficit with her courage and intellect. He wouldn't mind having her covering his backside in a fight.

"Do you regret not becoming a Marine?"

"Not as much since you hired me. I get to hone my skills at the office training center, and recently, I've had plenty of brushes with death to keep me on top of my game." She shot him another wry smile. "Always something hopping when you Coopers are around."

"You have no idea," he said, thinking about all his family had been through over the past few years. "We used to be such a calm, quiet family."

She shook her head. "I doubt that."

Jesse's cell phone rang, giving them both a start. He fished the phone from his pocket. It was his brother Rick.

"Turn on the television," Rick ordered tersely.

"What channel?"

"Any of 'em."

Jesse picked up the TV remote from the coffee table and turned on the television. It was already tuned to a news channel.

"That's my father," Evie said, her voice tinted by surprise.

A pretty black television reporter out of Birmingham stood in the live shot next to the general, holding the microphone toward him as he spoke.

The general's tone was grim. "My daughter Rita and my wife are safe, but I'm worried about my younger daughter, Evelyn."

Evie grimaced at her father's use of her given name.

"What is he doing?" Jesse asked Rick.

"Just watch."

"She's gone missing and I have no idea where she is." Her father's voice trembled with despair.

"What is he doing?" Evie echoed Jesse's words. "He knows where I am. He just talked to me."

"Technically, he doesn't," Jesse murmured, his

heart sinking into the pit of his gut. "And this is a way to put the world on notice to keep an eye out for you."

So much for flying under the radar.

"Why would he put me in danger this way?" Evie asked.

Jesse didn't like the only answer that made sense, but she had a right to know what they were up against.

"Someone's gotten to him," he said.

EVIE PACED in front of the sofa, her stomach in knots. To her right, the television played on, the volume muted. The news broadcasters had moved on to a new story, but Jesse had left the television on in case there were any new developments.

"Does your father know who's been hiring the SSU?" he asked.

"I'm not a hundred percent sure," she admitted. "But I think not. He hasn't told me much at all, but from what he's let slip, I think General Ross is the one who knew the most."

Jesse nodded. "That's what Emmett Harlowe told us."

Evie made herself sit down on the coffee table in front of Jesse, folding her hands in her lap. She willed herself to mimic Jesse's serene confidence, even if she couldn't feel it. "Even if we were able to talk my father into sharing his part of the code, we still don't have General Ross's."

"Shannon and Gideon have been working with Lydia Ross to figure out who might have his copy of the code." Jesse's sister Shannon had spent a week with General Ross's widow almost two months earlier, helping her archive the general's possessions in anticipation of Lydia's move away from the private Gulf Coast island that had been in her family for generations.

Shannon's discovery of the coded journal had been an accident, although Jesse had admitted afterward that he'd sent his sister to Nightshade Island in hope that she'd discover why the three generals were of such interest to the SSU.

"Have they had any luck?" Evie asked.

"Not yet," Jesse admitted. "There weren't many people the general trusted. General Harlowe and your father, of course, and his wife. The only other person who seems a likely prospect is Gideon, but he swears the general didn't give him any sort of code."

Evie didn't know the big, quiet ex-Marine very well, but the Coopers seemed to trust him, mostly because he'd helped Shannon escape a trio of SSU mercenaries determined to use her as leverage to get their hands on General Ross's journal. Formerly the Nightshade Island caretaker, Gideon had been in need of a job, with skills well-suited to Cooper Security. Plus, Shannon Cooper was clearly nuts about him. It hadn't taken much coaxing to convince Jesse that Gideon would be an asset to the company.

"And Mrs. Ross doesn't have any idea who else her husband would have trusted with the code?" she asked.

"She says he became suspicious of almost everyone in the weeks before his death. Maybe he knew someone had gotten wind of his investigations. If anyone can figure it out, Shannon can. She's like a dog with a bone."

Evie smiled. "I won't tell her you used that particular description."

"Thank you." His return smile was uncharacteristically warm, charming enough to make her stomach turn a couple of flips.

Jesse leaned close to pick up the television remote control, his shoulder brushing against hers. Her heart jumped, and it took most of her control to keep from reacting to his accidental touch.

"They're repeating your father's interview." He clicked the mute button to turn up the volume again.

"She's gone missing and I have no idea where she is," her father was saying to the reporter. "She left with a bodyguard after the wedding and failed to show up for the reception. Now the bodyguard has disappeared."

"Do you think that's true?" she asked Jesse. "Do you think those men disposed of Wilson's body?"

"Maybe," Jesse answered, his gaze fixed on the television as if trying to read her father's mind.

"General," the reporter said, "you're the second retired military commander to make the news in the last three months. As viewers will remember, General Emmett Harlowe, a retired Air Force general, went missing in late August, along with his wife and daughter. All three were safely recovered but remain under protection, their abduction as yet unsolved. Do you believe your daughter's disappearance could be connected?"

"I'm hoping my daughter is safe somewhere." Her father gazed directly into the camera. "Evie, if you're watching, remember how much your mother and I love you."

"I still don't understand what he's doing here," she admitted aloud.

"He's talking directly to you," Jesse answered. "What's he telling you?"

She frowned, listening to her father's words more carefully.

"Do you remember that Christmas in Falls Church, when you rode your bicycle up and down Oak Street? You loved that bike, but you had so much trouble learning to ride. Remember?"

She glanced at Jesse, grimacing. "So I was a little klutzy at age six."

"But you never gave up," her father continued. "And I don't want you to give up now. Trust yourself—you know how to find the answers."

"That seems really specific," Jesse murmured.

"It does." She looked at her father's serious expression, trying to figure out why something about his demeanor seemed off-kilter. "He's blinking a lot. Like he's fighting tears. But his eyes are dry."

Jesse watched for a second as her father looked into the camera, even as the reporter wrapped up the interview. "You're right."

"I don't suppose there's a recorder connected to that TV?"

"There is, actually. After your father's interview aired the first time, I set the DVR to record the rest of this cable network's news shows for the night. I thought we might want to see it again."

"Can we replay it? I want to watch it again."

"Sure." Jesse bent close again, his shoulder brushing hers once more as he pulled a second re-mote from the coffee-table drawer. He pushed a few buttons and her father's interview started replaying.

"See the blinks?" she asked. "It's odd. They seemed almost—"

"Deliberate," he finished for her.

"You see it, too?"

He nodded, his lips curving slightly. "The wily old leatherneck."

"What?'

"He's blinking in Morse code."

Chapter Five

Evie leaned closer to the television. "You're right."

"You know Morse code?"

"Only a few letters," she admitted. "I used to know more but I'm rusty. Can you tell what he's saying?"

Jesse reversed and started the recording over. "It's amazing he can blink code and speak at the same time." Admiration tinged his voice.

"He's always been a multitasker," Evie said lightly, hiding her pleasure. It was an unexpected surprise to hear Jesse speak positively about her father, given their antagonistic relationship.

"Here we go." As her father started to answer the reporter's first question, Jesse muted the television. "I'm not such a multitasker." He answered the unspoken question in Evie's gaze. "The sound is distracting."

Her father's eyelids tapped out a cadence of slow and fast blinks. "It seems to be just words, not full sentences," Jesse said after a few seconds. "One of the words is *Espera.*"

"We knew they were involved."

Jesse nodded, his eyes narrowing to follow her father's blinks. "*Admin—administration.* Definitely *administration.*"

"You think the conspiracy could go all the way to the president?"

"I'm not sure your father knows who. Just where to look."

"What else is he saying?" she asked a moment later when Jesse didn't say anything more.

"*Ruthless,*" he answered. "*Deadly.*" Jesse met her troubled gaze. "The last thing he spells out is *be very careful.*"

She stared back at him, shocked by her father's message. "He *wants* us to investigate the Espera Group?"

"I don't think he wants *us* to," Jesse answered quietly. "I think he wants *me* to, and he's giving me a place to start."

"You mean D.C.?"

He nodded. "It's where it all started, right? We know there's someone high in the government pulling strings for the Espera Group. Thanks to my brother-in-law Evan, we also know there are people in the Pentagon involved in all this, and your father worked at the Pentagon, right? That's why you and your family were living in D.C. when you were learning to ride your bike."

"Right. And the Espera Group is doing a lot of lobbying on Capitol Hill these days."

Jesse rose to his feet, his earlier calm control slipping away. He ran his hand over his crisp dark hair, frustration burning in his brown eyes. "We should have been looking there long before now. I don't know why we don't already have a crew in D.C. sniffing around."

"You've had a few fires here in Alabama to put out," Evie pointed out. "The SSU was here, causing a hell of a lot of trouble."

"What if that was part of their goal? To distract us, to keep us too busy to look closer at the genesis of this whole conspiracy?" He was pacing now, long, agitated strides that made her uneasy to watch.

Odd, being suddenly the calm one while Jesse lost his cool in front of her. Even during his romance with Rita, Jesse had been centered and unflappable, handling her sister's occasional meltdowns with remarkable maturity. Evie supposed being the eldest of six motherless children had made Jesse grow up quickly. So it was a little unnerving to watch him unraveling before her very eyes.

"So what if it was?" she asked, standing to block his steps.

He faltered to a stop, looking down at her with fathomless eyes. "So what if it was?"

"You've learned a hell of a lot about the SSU over the past few months. You know they've reconstituted themselves as AfterAssets. Your family has helped put several of them out of commission. You found out about my father and the other two generals and got your hands on that journal the SSU wants so badly. They're not winning this war. You are."

He put his hands on her shoulders. "I should have hired you years ago, Evelyn Marsh."

She grimaced at his use of her given name. "Please."

He smiled. "Evie." He gave her shoulders a quick squeeze and let go, turning away. He walked over to the window and shifted the curtain aside. The darkness outside the house and the light from within turned the window into a mirror that bounced their reflection back at them. Before Jesse dropped the curtain back into place, Evie caught a quick glimpse of his face in the glass, caught the hint of anxiety in his expression before he turned back to face her with a blank countenance.

"There's a big thrift store in Borland," he told her. "We'll drive over there in the morning to shop for clothes and supplies. I've got an emergency fund I can get my hands on in the morning, but it's got to stretch a long way."

"How long do you think we'll be staying here?"

"Here? Probably through tomorrow."

"Then what?"

"Then I'm going to find a new safe house for you and assign my brothers and sisters to take turns guarding you." He turned off the lamp near the window and started toward the hallway.

She followed him, frowning. He hadn't mentioned himself among her guards. "And where will you be when I'm in the new safe house?"

He turned so suddenly she had to catch herself on the doorframe to keep from plowing into him. His eyes gleamed black in the low light.

"I'm going to Washington, D.C."

"YOU'RE NOT LEAVING ME here," Evie declared as she followed him out to the car the next morning. "I can be an asset. I know the Washington area about as well as anyone. We lived there for years, even part of the time while my father was deployed overseas. I went to the first three years of high school there, learned to drive on the streets of the capital—"

"People will be looking for you, Evie. Your father made sure of that." Her father's televised plea meant that ordinary people, people who wouldn't normally pose a risk, would be a threat to revealing their location.

Why had Baxter Marsh put his daughter in such a position? It didn't make any sense. And then to give them a message where to look—it was insane. Unless—

"You just have to be the lone wolf, don't you?"

He looked over the roof of the car at Evie, who glared back at him, her blue eyes ablaze. "It's not about going to Washington alone. It's about going there without you."

"You think I'd be a liability?"

Secret Intentions

Damn it. Now she looked hurt.

But maybe he should let her think that was his reason. Let her go to the new safe house and lick her wounds for a day or two. Get good and pissed off at him so that she was glad he'd gone to Washington without her.

"That's not why," she said slowly, the injured look clearing from her face, replaced by dawning understanding. "You don't want to risk my getting hurt. Or worse."

"Can you imagine the hell I'd catch from your father if I took you with me and something happened?" He opened the car door and slid behind the steering wheel. "He didn't want you to go to D.C., Evie."

She buckled her seat belt. "So you don't think his Morse code message was to me?"

"Do you? Really?" He buckled his own belt and started the engine before he turned to look at her again. "Why would he make sure that your face was plastered all over the national news if he wanted you to sneak off to Washington, D.C.?"

"But the code—"

"You don't really know Morse code. Your father would know that."

"But you do. And he'd know that, too."

Jesse nodded. "He meant that message for me. And he made sure you were too high-profile to go with me."

"So we just let him have his way?"

"His way makes sense."

Her voice sharpened. "His way will get you killed."

Jesse shot her a wry smile. "Win-win for him."

"Don't say that."

"I'm not his favorite person."

"But he's not evil. He wouldn't deliberately set you up to get killed."

He touched her arm. "I was kidding."

"I'm not. You need backup in D.C. and I can do that."

He cut the engine and turned to look at her. "Evie, you're an accountant. You work at a computer all day. You're not an agent."

"I've been trained like an agent."

"Don't get cocky, Marsh. You received basic training. Agents go through many more weeks of training, plus annual refresher courses in case new procedures and weapons come into use."

"So give me a crash course in what I need to know."

If he wasn't so intent on keeping her safe, he'd admire her determination. "There's not nearly enough time."

"Give me a shot. I'm a fast learner."

"Evie—" He couldn't hold back a soft laugh. "What am I going to do with you?"

"Take me with you," she said.

He leaned toward her, catching her face between his hands. He'd meant it simply as a way to make her focus and listen to what he was saying, but the moment she looked up at him, blue eyes smoldering, he forgot his argument.

She was really stunning, with her porcelain skin and cornflower eyes. Rita was prettier, her attractiveness more blatant, impossible to miss, but Evie was the one with depth to her beauty. It was more than the fine bone structure or the perfect skin. It was the intellect in her bright eyes, the kindness in her frequent smiles.

Rita had been like a bright light, obscuring everything around her whenever she was in the room. Somehow, her luminance had made him completely miss the deeper, quieter appeal of her little sister.

He dropped his hands from Evie's face, feeling vulnerable and out of control. "Let's just go shopping. We have the rest of the day to work all of this out."

She was quiet during the twenty-minute drive to Borland. Too quiet. He ended up turning on the radio to fill the uncomfortable silence, fiddling around until he found a news station out of Birmingham.

The big news seemed to be Alabama and Auburn football, but at the half hour, the news broadcaster did mention Evie's disappearance. "Police are looking for Marsh and her bodyguard, Alan Wilson of Southland Security, neither of whom have been seen since yesterday. Wilson, a married father of two, worked for several years as a Jefferson County jail guard before taking the job with Southland."

Evie made a low moaning sound. "Married father of two."

"You didn't kill him."

"I still feel horrible."

The thrift store in Borland was huge, filling a space that had once been a large grocery store. Jesse stuck close to Evie while she shopped for clothes, mostly jeans and T-shirts, a few long-sleeved T-shirts and a couple of cardigans. "Will I need heavy winter clothes?" she asked quietly. "I mean, how long will I be keeping a low profile?"

"Get a sweater or two," he suggested.

She did as he suggested, adding a lined windbreaker to the pile, as well. Shoes came next, sneakers and boots, plus a couple of dressier flats that hadn't seen too much wear.

"You're going to need those at the safe house?" he asked in a low tone, keeping an eye out for other shoppers close enough to hear.

She gave him an enigmatic look and moved on to a different section of the store. She grabbed a couple of large water bottles and added them to their cart. "Can never have too many of these."

He eyed her suspiciously. "You're not thinking about the safe house at all, are you?"

"Shh," she said, glancing at a passing shopper.

"We'll talk later, remember?" She took charge of the cart and rolled it forward, leaving him to catch up.

They finished shopping and paid. On the way out to the car, Jesse handed her the keys. "Can you put the stuff in the backseat? I need to take a quick detour." He headed down the sidewalk toward the drugstore a couple of stores away. Inside, he found the item he wanted and carried it to the checkout counter, ignoring the clerk's curious look.

Evie gave him an equally curious look when he got back to the car and dropped the shopping bag on the seat between them. "What was that about?"

He nodded at the bag. "Thought you might need that."

She looked inside, then looked up at him, a question in her blue eyes.

"You're too recognizable," he said. "And because I know damned well you plan to go to D.C. no matter how you have to do it, I figure you have a better chance staying under the radar as a redhead."

Evie grinned as she pulled the box of hair dye from the bag. "You won't regret this."

"I already do," he murmured, starting the car.

But if she was going to risk her neck by going to Washington, he was going to make damned sure he was there to watch her back.

THE SUPER BUDGET MOTEL near Christiansburg, Virginia, wasn't the nicest place Evie had ever seen, but it had two things going for it—clean beds and free Wi-Fi. Jesse had made it clear, when they'd decided to stop rather than push on to D.C. Monday evening, they were going to share a room.

"We'll find a place with two beds," he'd said, "but I'm not comfortable with being in a separate room when there are people trying to kidnap you."

"They won't even recognize me," she'd argued, tugging at the now-short auburn hair framing her face.

"Not taking a chance." His tone ended the discussion.

She wouldn't have protested at all, she thought, if she weren't still so bloody vulnerable to her attraction to him. Maybe it was just a crush, but knowing so didn't change much. He was still the sexiest man she'd ever met, and if he took her face between his hands again, the way he had in the car the day before, she wasn't sure she'd keep her cool a second time.

"I'm going to take a shower. Do you want to go first?"

"Go ahead," she said. "Can I borrow your computer?"

"Sure."

He didn't hesitate, she noticed. In fact, he seemed to be going out of his way to accommodate her on this trip. It was as if, once he'd decided to let her tag along, he was buttering her up for something.

Probably about to toss some onerous ground rules her way. Jesse was big on ground rules.

"What's your password?" she called as he disappeared into the bathroom just as the log-in screen came up on the computer.

He stepped back out, already stripped down to his jeans. "It's jf2Rdx378. The *R* is capitalized."

She dragged her gaze away from his powerful shoulders and flat belly to type the code into the computer. Jesse went back into the bathroom, and a few moments later, the shower came on.

Don't think about him naked, she told herself as she pulled up the web browser and typed in *Espera Group.*

Several pages of links came up in response to her search. She scrolled through them, having read most of them before now. She was looking for something new. Something more informative than the slick, PR-oriented doublespeak she had found on most of her searches.

She came across an anti–Espera Group weblog on the second page of links and clicked. The blog design was crude and amateur, but whoever ran the site wrote with passion, even if his style was occasionally on the clunky side and his grammar faltered now and then.

"If the Cambridge administration pushes for the treaty, and can strong-arm enough congressmen to go along with it, he'll win the accolades of his party and the gratitude of the world," the blogger began.

"He'll also guarantee that the world's oil will be controlled not by individual countries vulnerable to both carrots and sticks but to an unaccountable, unleverageable group of nameless, faceless bureaucrats with no track record of wisdom, responsibility or mercy."

Evie couldn't argue with his point. For decades, people had been trying to figure out how to fix the oil problem. The resource was used as a bargaining tool, fought for, killed for, rationed and vilified because the countries that needed the most of it had to walk softly around the mercurial, often despotic countries that controlled most of it.

People were tired of being held hostage to the whims of dictators sitting on a fortune in black gold. The solution the Espera Group was selling would seem like the perfect answer to a whole lot of them. Sharing the oil evenly and equitably, controlling production for the sake of conservation and reducing waste, taking the reins out of the hands of people who wielded oil like a weapon—what was there not to like?

But who made the decisions? The multinational group favored by the Espera Group, handpicked by their supporters? That kind of "consensus" rarely worked out to the benefit of those who played by the rules. And the lack of transparency guaranteed that corruption would take root.

Near the end of the blog post was a link. "Think I'm overreacting to a treaty that hasn't even been presented to Congress? Take a look just how deep the rot in the current administration goes."

Jesse emerged from the bathroom in a clean pair of jeans, a towel around his neck only partially hiding his bare, still-damp chest. His dark hair was still wet, rivulets running down his lean cheeks. He brought the towel up and ran it over his hair, his chest muscles flexing.

"There's still plenty of hot water left if you want to take a turn," he said, crossing to the bed next to the table where she sat. He sat on the edge and nodded at the page she had open. "What are you looking at?"

"No Espera," she answered, dragging her gaze back to the computer screen. "It's an anti–Espera Group blog. He's pretty eloquent in opposition to the Wolfsburg Treaty," Evie said. "He may even know more about who's behind the group than we do."

"A blogger?"

"You'd be surprised how deep some of these bloggers' resources go. It looks as if he's based in Arlington, Virginia, so he's right there near D.C. He may know people intimately involved in the decision-making process."

"Does he give his name?"

"No. A lot of bloggers prefer to remain anonymous."

"Probably thinks the government is out to get him."

She frowned at Jesse's dismissive tone. "He might be right."

Jesse dropped the damp towel onto the bed beside him, giving her a skeptical look. "And he might be typing away in his mother's basement, surrounded by his sci-fi action figures."

"Jerk," she muttered, clicking the link at the bottom of the blog post. After a brief wait, she got a "Page not found" message. "Hmm."

Jesse moved closer, bending to read over her shoulder. "A broken link from a blogger. What a shock."

Damn, he smelled good. Soap-and-water fresh, with a hint of pure masculinity underlying the clean scent. She dragged her mind back to the topic. "You're an old-media snob."

He laughed. "I just know you can't trust everything you read on the internet. How old is that blog post?"

She went back to the blog page. "It was posted a week ago."

"And that's the last post on the page?" He sounded surprised. "Issue bloggers usually post at least once a day, if not more."

"Maybe he's on vacation or something." She turned around to look at Jesse. He stood close, still shirtless and unspeakably attractive on a purely visceral level.

"Without getting a guest blogger to fill in?" Jesse sat back on the edge of the bed again and picked up the black T-shirt lying on the comforter beside him. Evie bit back a sigh as he slipped the shirt over his head, covering his bare chest.

"I don't know. Maybe he had some sort of family emergency and had to bug out for a bit."

"Well, let me have the laptop awhile. I need to download some of my files on the SSU and the Espera Group from the Cooper Security web archive. Go take a shower and we'll walk down to the burger joint on the corner to get something to eat." He traded places with her, waving toward the bathroom.

When she emerged from the shower, dressed in fresh jeans and a long-sleeved T-shirt she'd purchased at the thrift store, she found Jesse lying on the bed by the window, staring up at the ceiling. He turned his head as she entered the room, his dark eyes following her movements as she settled on the edge of the other bed.

His silent regard made her feel awkward. "Did you get everything downloaded okay?" she asked.

"Yeah." He continued to look at her thoughtfully.

She squelched the urge to check her reflection in the mirror to see if she had a smudge on her face. "Good."

"I've been thinking, though."

She lifted her eyebrows. "Is that good or bad?"

He smiled. "I'm not sure. I was thinking about your blogger friend."

"Well, it's not like I actually know him—"

"I did a little looking around. Found his real identity. It's a kid named Shawn Bellington. Lived in Arlington Heights."

"Lived?"

Jesse sat up. "I did a web search for his name and found an obituary. He was killed in a hit-and-run accident a week ago."

Chapter Six

"Wow." Evie looked uneasy. "That's weird, isn't it?"

"Could be a coincidence." Jesse held out his hand to help her up. "Meanwhile, there are burgers and fries to be eaten."

She took his hand, smiling up at him. "And a chocolate shake?"

He squeezed her hand before letting go. "After the last few days you've had, I think you've earned it."

They discussed Shawn Bellington's death a little more over dinner, without coming to any solid conclusion about whether it was a coincidence or another notch in the SSU's belt. Jesse was prone to think the former, but he could tell Evie wasn't convinced.

After dinner back at the motel, Jesse called his brother Rick again to check on things at home. He was relieved to be able to tell Evie that her family was still safe. "Rita and her husband checked in from Spain. Everything's still fine. Rick says your father relented and let Cooper Security send a couple of agents to Spain to supplement the security people who already accompanied them."

"Poor Rita," Evie said with a faint smile. "Honeymooning with her new husband and an entourage of nosy security guards watching their every move. Yeah, I bet they're having the time of their lives."

"It's necessary."

"I know. It's also sort of horrifying to imagine."

"Rick sent a male/female team. They're posing as fellow newlyweds, so hopefully their presence will be a little less intrusive."

Evie cocked her head to one side, studying him for a long, silent moment. He returned the favor, taking in her newly changed appearance. She looked good as a redhead, the color perfect for her pale complexion and deep blue eyes. The short, choppy cut suited her as well, though she'd already told him she was going to find a hair salon as soon as they got to Washington to get her self-inflicted haircut cleaned up by a professional.

Personally, he thought she'd done a creditable job. Her thick hair was blunt cut to chin level, showing off her long, slender neck. It was a cut that should have made her look even younger than her twenty-seven years, but something about the look gave her an added air of maturity.

She definitely wasn't a little girl anymore.

"Does it bother you?" she asked.

He realized he had no idea what she was asking.

Somewhere, in his contemplation of her appearance, he'd completely lost track of their conversation. "Does what bother me?"

"Thinking about Rita being married."

"Oh." How to answer that? He'd gone to the wedding expecting the idea to bother him greatly, but to his surprise, he'd discovered he'd made peace with losing Rita for good. "I'm happy if she's happy."

Her lips curved in a crooked half smile. "That's a very careful answer."

"It's true, though. She seemed happy. So I'm good with it. It's what I wanted for her, you know. Always. I wanted her to be happy."

"Because you love her."

"There's a lot to love about Rita. You know that better than anyone."

Evie nodded. "I do know. And she *is* happy."

"Then I'm glad."

Evie looked down at her hands a moment, as if she had something more she wanted to say. But when she looked up at him again, her expression was neutral, save for a slight smile. "Can I borrow your computer again? I wanted to do a little more nosing around before bedtime."

Bedtime, Jesse thought. Until now, the two of them had stayed busy enough to postpone thinking about what bedtime meant.

It should have meant nothing. Two friends sharing a room for the night. No big deal.

Except it suddenly seemed like a huge deal. All

evening long, whether he'd been leaning over her shoulder to read the blog she'd found or walking side by side with her to the burger joint down the block, Jesse had found himself acutely aware of Evie Marsh. Not as a friend or a colleague but as an attractive, sexually tempting woman.

He hadn't spent the past twelve years in a celibate homage to the girl that got away, but the busy days and nights at Cooper Security for the past six months had kept him well out of the dating pool. It had been a long time since he'd shared a dinner alone with a woman, even one as public as a booth in the corner of a burger joint. It had been even longer since he'd spent the night in the same room with a woman.

So don't think of Evie as a woman.

Yeah. Right.

"Can I use the laptop?" Evie asked again, cocking her head slightly as she narrowed her gaze at him.

"Oh, yeah. Sure." Giving himself a quick mental kick, he scooted down the bed, out of her way. She settled on the edge of his bed next to him, smelling like the herbal shower gel the motel supplied for guests. It was cheap stuff, but somehow on Evie it smelled like Gossamer Mountain after a spring rain.

God, that was lame. He had to get ahold of himself before he blew this mission completely.

He was sitting too close to her. All those pheromones or whatever were going straight to his head, sapping his focus. He took advantage of her instant absorption with the laptop to walk across the room, putting necessary distance between them.

He settled on the other bed with his back to her and checked his email on his phone. Mostly work-related odds and ends he quickly delegated. One email from Megan telling him that she'd already heard from Delilah and Terry, the agents he'd assigned to keep an eye on Rita and her new husband in Barcelona. Everything was quiet in Spain, for now.

He glanced over his shoulder at Evie. She'd settled back on his bed with her legs crossed, his notebook computer balanced on her lap. She didn't lift her head to return his gaze, completely focused on whatever she was reading.

Jesse tamped down his curiosity. If she found something he needed to know, she'd tell him. Going back over there to read over her shoulder would be nothing but an excuse to get close to her again.

He kicked off his shoes and settled on her bed, resting his tense neck against the bed pillows. Maybe he should do a little web crawling of his own, see what else he could find out about the Espera Group.

ON THE CHANCE that the site had been down only temporarily, Evie tried the link at the end of the

No Espera blog. But once again, it went to an error page. So much for that idea.

Sticking with the *No Espera* blog, she clicked through the list of links in the blog's sidebar until she came across another anti–Espera Group blog called *Esperatopia*. This blog's tone was breezier and more sarcastic than *No Espera*'s more measured, academic treatment of the subject. But in the midst of the witty snark and the occasional profanity, she discovered a post, dated around the time of the *No Espera* post with the missing link, that not only mentioned the now-dead link but provided a screen grab of the page that had disappeared into cyberspace.

At first glance, Evie didn't see why the bloggers thought the link was such a big deal. It was merely the text of a speech from two years earlier, given by the current secretary of energy before he had been chosen for that position by President Cambridge last year. The first half was dry and pedantic, outlining the benefits and drawbacks of alternative energy sources. Evie found herself in danger of nodding off as she scanned the material, looking for any mention of the Espera Group and its support of the Wolfsburg Treaty.

She found it near the end of the speech.

For too many decades, under both parties, the United States has made ourselves hostages to the whims and dictates of some of the world's most depraved power brokers. Even as we strive to develop and implement alternative sources of energy, we must not be naive. It may take decades, even centuries, to economically replace our dependence on fossil fuels.

For this reason, the free-thinking, freedom-loving nations of the world must unite to regulate the production, sale and consumption of our world's most vital resource.

Evie sat back from the laptop, goose bumps scattering across her arms and legs. "Jesse?"

He looked up from his phone, his eyes narrowing at the sound of alarm in her voice. "Did you find something?"

"Ever heard of Morris Gamble?"

Jesse nodded. "Secretary of Energy. Why?"

"Because I think he may be a member of the Espera Group."

AT THE SOUND of Maddox Heller's sleepy voice, Jesse checked his watch and saw, with dismay, that it was after midnight. "Sorry about the late hour," he said, "but I need your help."

As he outlined the events of the past two days to his silent partner at Cooper Security, he couldn't keep his gaze from wandering across the room to Evie, who lay on the other bed, watching him with a solemn expression.

"We've discovered a possible connection be-

tween the Espera Group and Secretary of Energy
Morris Gamble. It's nebulous at the moment, but
we've been suspicious all along that the SSU had
connections high in the government. What if it's
Gamble? What if he's a true believer in what the
Espera Group is peddling, and he's not afraid to
spend a little cash to manipulate people and situations to get what they want?"

"Gamble would be closer to the president in
terms of influence than Barton Reid was, for sure,"
Heller agreed in his still-sleepy Southern drawl, re-
ferring to the former State Department official who
had paid the SSU to be his own private army as he
manipulated political situations in several countries
to his own benefit. "We've thought for a while that
Reid was acting more as the general, directing the
troops in the field while someone higher-up was
calling all the shots, right?"

"Yes, but we were leaning toward someone in
the CIA, based on the threats against Amanda."
Earlier that year, a group of SSU agents had made
an attempt on the life of a beautiful former CIA
agent his brother Rick had fallen in love with years
earlier. Turning up in the right place at the wrong
time, Rick had helped Amanda escape, and while
on the run together, they'd rekindled their former
relationship.

They'd also figured out that the SSU assassins
must have had at least some help from someone in
the CIA, because her whereabouts were known by

only a handful of people in the agency where she'd formerly worked. Amanda's former CIA handler, Alexander Quinn, had as much as said there was someone at the CIA pulling a few strings for Barton Reid and the SSU.

Jesse sat up straighter. "Heller, where's Alexander Quinn these days? You have any idea?"

"I know he's stateside. I can get in touch with him if you need me to. What do you have in mind?"

"If Gamble is connected to the Espera Group, would Quinn know?"

"I'd bet he might already have a few suspicions at least."

"Can you put me in touch with him? You can give him this phone number. It's untraceable to me."

"Sure, but do you really want to deal with Quinn? You know he has his own agenda for everything. I can't promise you he won't run you straight into a big ol' mess."

Jesse smiled at Heller's understatement. "Big ol' mess" didn't come close to describing the sort of trouble Alexander Quinn could get a person into, but the wily spy might be Jesse's only chance to find out who was pulling the strings in Washington.

He slanted another look at Evie, his wry amusement quickly fading. Dealing with Quinn might be a chance he was willing to take for himself, but could he risk putting Evie into even more danger?

"Let me call you back in the morning," Jesse said. "I need to discuss it with Evie first."

"I'll try to track down Quinn first thing in the a.m. What time will you call back?"

"Let's say eight. We have a long drive ahead of us tomorrow and I'd like to get things settled early."

"Talk to you then."

Jesse hung up and met Evie's curious gaze. "Alexander Quinn?" she asked.

"CIA agent."

"I know who he is. You can't work at Cooper Security for two weeks, much less two months, without hearing how he threw Rick and Amanda together last spring. But why do we want to talk to him?"

"Quinn is working stateside these days. Probably in D.C., although Heller didn't say that specifically."

"Heller? You're not talking about Maddox Heller, are you?"

Jesse realized Evie didn't know about Heller's involvement in Cooper Security. Few outside of his own family did. "Heller's my silent partner at Cooper Security. He owns over half the company."

Evie's eyes widened. "I thought it belonged to you and your family."

"We're buying it back with the profits," Jesse said. "Maddox had the seed money and the idea for the company, and he tapped me to run it and be its front man."

"And he couldn't be the face of the company because of his reputation," Evie guessed. "Who'd put their trust in a guy whose claim to fame is letting a woman die in front of him without lifting a finger?"

Jesse could tell from Evie's tone that she'd bought into the official story. "It's not that simple," he said flatly. "Heller was protecting a group of U.S. Embassy employees during the rebel siege in Kaziristan." Several years earlier, al Adar rebels had taken control of the U.S. Embassy in the central Asian country of Kaziristan, killing as many embassy personnel as they could find. "He and the others were trying to escape the rebels without being seen. If Heller had done anything to save that interpreter, he'd have risked the lives of a dozen other people."

Evie looked surprised. "But he was dishonorably discharged. His name has practically become synonymous with cowardice in uniform."

"Barton Reid made sure of that. He scapegoated Heller to make sure nobody looked too closely at his behavior during the siege." Jesse tamped down a sudden flood of indignant rage at the thought of how thoroughly Reid and a handful of gullible State Department investigators had discredited a good Marine. "But it's too late to clear Heller's name now. He's made peace with it. He has a good life, a pretty wife and a cute kid. And Cooper Security's making a little extra money for him."

"Still, if what you say is true—"

"It's true," Jesse said flatly.

"Then his name should be cleared. I can't imagine anything worse for a Marine than to be thought dishonorable and cowardly." The outrage blazing from Evie's blue eyes echoed Jesse's own anger at the terrible miscarriage of justice against his friend.

"I've tried to talk him into making a bigger stink about it, but I don't think he wants to be in the public eye that way again." Jesse sat on the edge of his own bed, facing her. "Back to Quinn—Heller can put me in contact with him if that's what I want."

"You think he may know more about the Espera Group and maybe even Morris Gamble than he's let anyone know so far?"

"Even if he doesn't have any proof to offer, he may have suspicions. And suspicions can lead to proof eventually, right?"

She nodded, although he could tell from the shuttered look on her face that she had doubts. "Quinn's ruthless. I've heard horror stories from Amanda."

"Ruthless, yes. But he's a patriot. And even though I'm not a big fan of his methods, I know he'll do whatever he thinks is necessary to protect this country. That's what I want, too. I'm willing to risk it."

"You're using 'I' a lot." Her chin lifted and her gaze locked with his. "Planning to ditch me?"

"I think you should consider going into witness protection." Even as he said the words, a part of him rebelled against the thought of letting her out of his sight. He didn't trust anyone else to keep her safe, he realized. It wasn't arrogance on his part that made him feel that way; he knew he was as prone to making mistakes as anyone.

But he cared enough about her to risk anything to keep her safe. It was personal to him in a way it wouldn't be to other bodyguards he might assign to keep her out of harm's way.

"No," she said firmly. "No way."

He wasn't surprised. She'd survived two kidnapping attempts, seen a man killed right before her eyes, and she wanted justice. He might wish she weren't the sort of woman who'd want to help deliver that justice herself, but he had to admire her for her raw courage and determination. "It's going to get a lot more dangerous before it's over."

"I owe it to my family." Evie twisted her hands in her lap, looking terrified but resolute. "And to Alan Wilson's wife and kids. I don't know if they'll ever find a body to bury, all because somebody was after me and my family. The least I can do is be part of proving why it happened and maybe, just maybe, bringing the perpetrators to justice."

"You're an accountant, Evie. This kind of work requires skills."

"So you teach me everything you know."

"Between now and the time we get to D.C.?"

"Do the best you can, hotshot." She managed a cheeky grin that faded all too quickly into worry.

A daunting task, he thought, to try to prepare her over the course of a few hours for what they might find when they arrived at the capital. But there were a few lessons he could teach her, ways to put her into the mind-set, at least, to handle the unexpected.

He just hoped it would be enough to keep them both alive.

Chapter Seven

Farragut Square Park was busy at midday on a Tuesday, workers from nearby buildings mingling with tourists who had their noses buried deep in D.C. maps. Jesse had memorized the D.C. map while Evie drove, determined not to look like a tourist. And he had Evie, whose memories of Washington hadn't faded much over the intervening years.

She'd loved living in Washington, flaws and all. She'd enjoyed the hectic pace, the silly self-importance of its political class, the awe-inspiring sense of history to be found in its alabaster monuments and majestic landmarks. Even though she had no pressing desire to return there to live again, now that she'd settled into the slower pace of life in Chickasaw County, Alabama, she was grateful for the experience of living in the nation's capital for most of her childhood and youth.

"Where did Quinn tell you he'd meet us?" she asked as they walked down the sidewalk outside the park. Ahead to the right, inside the chains delineating the park, the statue of Admiral David Farragut rose on his white stone pedestal, drawing the attention of camera-snapping tourists who ringed the statue to get a quick shot of the Civil War Navy hero.

"He said to look for the Army and Navy Club Building on 17th Street."

She pointed toward a tall, brown brick building with black iron minibalconies under some of the tall, rectangular windows. "That's it." Her father had been a member. He'd taken her and Rita to eat lunch in the main dining room at the club a few times when they were old enough to behave politely. He'd also treated Evie to dinner at the club when she learned she'd earned a full-ride scholarship to Vanderbilt University.

"He said we should go to a bench across from the Army and Navy Club Building." He pointed toward four black iron benches flanking the narrow concrete path leading into the park. Only one was occupied at the moment, by a homeless man in ragged clothing who slouched against the bench back, sporadically reaching into a paper sack beside him and tossing its contents—birdseed, Evie discerned—to the crowd of pigeons fluttering around his feet.

The man looked up suddenly, his gaze connecting with hers. The intensity of his stare made her breath catch.

She closed her fingers around Jesse's wrist. "Jesse."

He followed her gaze. "That's Quinn."

"Are you sure?" She gave the homeless man another quick look. He had a day's growth of beard, a gaunt look of hunger, as if he hadn't eaten a solid meal in days. His clothes were worn and dirty, and the shoes on his feet were riddled with holes and stains.

"He's a CIA agent. He's good with the disguises." Jesse twined his fingers with hers and crossed to the bench. "Mind if we sit?" he asked.

Quinn looked down at the pigeons. "Don't scare away the birds."

"Wouldn't dream of it," Jesse murmured. He put Evie on the outside of the bench and settled between her and Quinn. "Nice getup."

"Worked hours for this look," Quinn murmured. "Heller says you suspect Morris Gamble is involved with the Espera Group."

"I do."

"He's not influential enough to help them push the treaty," Quinn said, his tone dismissive.

"Are you suggesting we pack up and go back home?" Jesse's tone was low but fierce.

"I'm saying you need to look a little deeper than Secretary Gamble." Quinn held out the bag to Jesse. "Seeds for the birds?"

"I'm not a big fan of your cryptic hogwash." Jesse reached into the bag. His hand went still a moment, then came back out, curled into a fist. He opened his palm halfway and Evie saw, in the middle of a small mound of birdseed, a slip of paper with a phone number written on it.

She looked up at Quinn. He met her gaze, a slight smile curving his lips. "Lots of parties go on here in D.C. Ever been to one?"

"A few," she said carefully.

"Lucky you." Quinn tossed birdseed to the birds at his feet. Four pigeons grappled for the morsels, wings flapping.

"Call the number tonight after six. You'll find out what to do next." Quinn stood up, handing the bag of seeds to Evie. "Be sure to feed them all the grain." He staggered away, favoring one leg and looking for all the world like a homeless man, drunk and down on his luck.

She reached into the bag and found there was only a handful of birdseed left. As she scooped it into her palm to toss to the pigeons, she felt something cold and metal against her fingertips.

She glanced at Jesse.

"What?" he asked.

She withdrew her hand, the birdseed still nestled in the closed palm. She tossed the seeds to the pigeons and handed Jesse the bag. "Looks like it's all gone. Can you check and see?"

He gave her an odd look but opened the bag and looked inside. His only reaction was a slight lift of his dark eyebrows. "You hungry?" He nodded toward the street, where a food truck had pulled up to the curb. Pedestrians had already detoured from the sidewalk and the park to line up in front of the service window.

She hadn't eaten at a food truck in a long time. "It's a gamble," she warned him. "Very hit-or-miss."

"I'm not afraid to take a risk." He folded the paper bag into a neat square and stuck it in the front pocket of his jeans. "Let's go before the line gets too long."

Evie found her patience growing short as they waited in line to order from the bright blue truck painted in big white letters that read "Levantino." Its menu, painted on a board hung out on the side of the truck, boasted a variety of Middle Eastern favorites.

Jesse ordered a lamb pita, while Evie opted for a falafel pita wrap. They ate as they walked toward the Metro station on the corner.

"Jesse—"

He caught her hand, squeezing it gently. "Let's talk when we get back to the motel." He held on to her hand all the way to the Metro station, letting go only when they had to toss the remains of their lunch before getting on the train.

The ride to the Virginia Square Metro station was short but frustratingly tense for Evie, who had a million questions about their brief but eventful encounter with Alexander Quinn. She held her tongue until they reached their motel room.

"What kind of key is that?" she asked as soon as the door shut behind them, closing them safely inside the small, neat room. She flicked on the light and met Jesse's dark gaze.

"I'm not sure." Jesse pulled the paper bag from his pocket, unfolded it and dumped the contents on the dresser top. A few stray seeds spilled out along with the brass key Evie had found inside the bag when she was feeding the pigeons.

"It looks like a house key." She picked it up and examined it, frowning as she spotted something etched in the metal. She turned on the dresser lamp and held the key under the light for a better view.

"'AJH,'" Jesse said, reading over her shoulder.

"Does that mean anything to you?" she asked.

"Not off the top of my head." He took the key from her, his fingers brushing lightly over hers. She tamped down a shiver as he examined the key, turning it over a couple of times as if seeking more clues.

"Typical Quinn," he said finally. "Gives you half a clue and walks away."

"What about the number?"

He pulled the slip of paper from his other pocket and unfolded it. "Looks like a local phone number."

"Is there anything on the back?"

He turned it over and found something written in faint pencil scratching. His lips curved. "'Mention Mad Dog,'" he read.

"Mad Dog?" she asked, utterly confused.

He looked at her, the grin spreading. "It's a nickname. For Maddox Heller. Whoever belongs to this number must know Heller."

"Let's call it." She reached for the slip of paper.

He held it out of her reach, catching her outstretched hand. "Before we go a step further, let's be clear about this. Alexander Quinn does not have our best interests at heart."

"I know that."

"Whatever he's sending us into could get us killed."

She tried to ignore the sudden spread of goose bumps down her spine. "I know that, too."

He didn't speak for a moment, his gaze so intense she felt as if her knees would melt right out from under her. When he cupped his palm over the curve of her jaw, her breath faltered, trapped in her suddenly tight throat.

"I can still send you somewhere safe," he said in a low, sexy voice that sent a fresh series of shivers through her. "I can put you in protection and take it from here myself."

A part of her knew she should take him up on the offer. What did she know about the kind of skulduggery she and Jesse might be facing if they followed through on Alexander Quinn's cryptic clues?

But how could she leave Jesse to fend for himself? She was the one who knew this city, not Jesse.

She was the one the SSU had targeted. It was her problem, and she couldn't bear the idea of letting Jesse face the consequences alone while she hid from danger somewhere far away.

"You need me to watch your back."

His smile faded. "Tough little Evie Marsh. You always were my champion, weren't you?" His expression had gone serious. "Rita told me, you know. How you took our side in the arguments with your father. She appreciated your support more than you know."

She felt a flutter of guilt. She hadn't opposed her father because of Rita. Even then, when she'd been barely seventeen and too young and foolish to understand anything about love, she hadn't been able to bear the thought of Jesse Cooper walking out of their lives. When Rita broke things off with him only a year later, she hadn't been the only Marsh sister to cry herself to sleep.

She wasn't going to walk away from him now, no matter how much danger they were in.

"Let's do it." She squared her shoulders. "As soon as it's six, let's make the call."

JESSE COOPER WASN'T A MAN prone to the jitters. Long before he'd signed up with the Marine Corps, life, and his father's practical tutelage, had taught him that even the most challenging moments in life could be overcome or, barring that, endured if he dug his feet in and held his ground. Having his mother walk away when he was sixteen years old, leaving him to parent five younger siblings while his father worked long shifts at the sheriff's department, had taught him that life wasn't fair and nothing useful ever came from fretting about things he couldn't control.

But waiting for Evie Marsh to walk out of the bedroom where she was dressing had his nerves jangling.

If anyone had told him that day he'd staked out Rita Marsh's wedding that he'd be attending a black-tie dinner at the British ambassador's residence in D.C. a few short days later, he'd have laughed. But here he was, half-strangled by the bow tie around his neck and feeling like an idiot with a black silk cummerbund fastened around his waist, waiting for Evie to finish primping for the party.

"You look nervous. That's dangerous under the circumstances."

Jesse turned to face the tall, slim man who sat in an armchair in the corner of the living room, looking utterly relaxed, even bored. His name was Nicholas Darcy, and it had been his number Quinn had given them at the park. Getting a phone call out of the blue from a stranger had set him on edge, and mentioning Maddox Heller's name had eased his suspicion only marginally. But he'd agreed to meet with Jesse and Evie the evening before, even treat-

ing them to dinner at a nice restaurant in Georgetown before taking them to his apartment so they
could talk in private.

Darcy, it turned out, was a Diplomatic Security
Service agent. He had a hint of a British accent, despite being an American—a result of growing up in
the United Kingdom, he'd explained, the son of a
foreign-service official working out of the American Embassy in London.

Darcy had known Heller from his time at the
American Embassy in Tablis, Kaziristan. He'd later
run into the disgraced Marine again on the small
Caribbean island of Mariposa, where he'd been
working at the consulate while Heller was living
the life of a beach bum, licking the wounds left by
his dishonorable discharge.

"He met his wife there, you know," Darcy had
told them over decaf coffee in his Georgetown
apartment. "She was there for some paranormal
convention." Darcy smiled. "I shouldn't laugh. She
helped save a lot of people's lives while she was
there, at great risk to herself. If she wants to fancy
herself an empath, it's fine with me."

Evie had exchanged glances with Jesse at that
point. He shrugged, realizing there was a lot about
Maddox Heller he still didn't know.

Darcy had also examined the key Evie had found
in the sack of birdseed. "It looks like an apartment
key," he'd told them, turning the key over to study

the etchings. "'AJH,'" he'd said aloud. "Someone's initials?"

"Oh." Evie had given a little start, drawing the gaze of both men. "What if it's Ann Jeanette Harlowe? Maybe this key goes to Annie's apartment."

Annie Harlowe was the daughter of Air Force General Emmett Harlowe, who had disappeared for nearly a month back in mid-August, taken captive along with his wife and Annie by ruthless members of the SSU. Annie had managed to escape, and her parents were later released under mysterious circumstances. All three were now under protection in a Birmingham-area safe house, guarded by Cooper Security agents, including Jesse's younger brother Wade.

"You mean her apartment here in D.C.?" Jesse had been skeptical. "How will we ever find it?"

"I have the address," Evie told him. "At least, I can get it off our web archive. Cooper Security has been paying her bills for her while she's under our protection, remember?"

They'd found the apartment early this morning, a pretty resident-owned two-story flat in Arlington, less than a mile from the motel where they were staying. The key had fit.

And inside, to Evie's delight and Jesse's bemusement, they'd found a rolling clothes rack with several evening dresses in Evie's size, along with shoes and jewelry to choose from.

"What is this about?" Jesse had looked at Darcy for answers.

The DSS agent had smiled, although he didn't look particularly amused. "So that's what Quinn's call was about."

"What call?"

"Shortly before you called, Quinn contacted me. He wanted me to arrange two more invitations to the dinner party tonight at the British ambassador's residence. The Ambassador is an old family friend of mine."

"Why that party?" Evie had asked, dragging her attention away from the evening gowns.

"You said you wanted to learn more about Secretary Gamble, yes?" Darcy continued smiling, although he looked no happier. "Well, the secretary will be at the party tonight."

Procuring tickets, he'd told them, had been no trouble. He'd handed them over to Jesse and taken his leave to get ready for the party himself. He'd met them back at Annie Harlowe's apartment an hour ago, sharply dressed in a black silk tuxedo and carrying a tux for Jesse and a small envelope that he handed over to Evie.

Inside the envelope had been a driver's license and passport with Evie's photo—red hair and all—and the name "Evelyn Martin."

"How did you get that photo?" Jesse had asked.

"You don't think Quinn met you alone in that park, do you?" Darcy had handed the license and passport to Evie. "Keep them with you in case you ever need them."

Then he'd sent Evie off to dress while he and Jesse remained outside in the living room of Annie Harlowe's apartment, stewing in tense silence.

"You're taking a dangerous risk," Darcy commented.

"I'm aware of that."

"How sure are you that Gamble is connected to the Espera Group?" Darcy hadn't said so, but Jesse suspected the Diplomatic Security Service might be keeping an eye on the group, just as they watched other groups that might pose a threat to Americans abroad or foreign visitors in the States.

"Not sure at all," Jesse answered. "That's what I'm trying to ascertain."

Before Darcy could respond, the bedroom door opened and Evie emerged in a simple navy dress. The top part of the dress hugged her torso and showed off her white shoulders, while the skirt was sheer and floaty, swishing around her legs as she walked toward them.

"Good choice or not?" she asked. Jesse was surprised she sounded unsure of herself. Did she really not realize how beautiful she was?

"Stunning choice," Darcy said before Jesse could speak. Evie flashed him a bright smile that made Jesse want to knock the stupid grin off the DSS agent's handsome face.

"You look great," Jesse said, moving quickly to her side and offering his arm.

"You clean up pretty well yourself, Cooper," she responded with a lopsided grin that made his heart skip a beat. "So what happens now?"

"We crash a party," he answered.

Chapter Eight

Sir Henry Steed had taken over the top spot at the British Embassy only two years earlier, Darcy told Evie and Jesse during the limousine ride to the ambassador's residence that evening. He sat alone on the seat facing backward, while Jesse sat protectively close to Evie, as if he expected bullets to start flying through the limo's windows any moment. "Henry's been bucking for this promotion for decades," Darcy said. "He's a fine chap, very agreeable, but he's always found himself second-best until now."

"How did he manage to make it here this time?" Jesse asked.

Darcy smiled. "The previous ambassador made the mistake of getting a senator's daughter pregnant."

"Oh." Evie grimaced. "What should we know about the ambassador before we meet him?"

"He'll be charmed by you," Darcy said with a smile. "He has a soft spot for beautiful women."

"Thank you."

"Very nice," Jesse said in a flat tone, "but could you come up with something a little more helpful?"

Darcy slanted a look at him. "He's a big fan of American football. As you're from Alabama—you should be able to handle that topic, yes?"

"Absolutely," Evie answered brightly, trying to defuse the tension rising in the back of the limo. "Anything else?"

"Actually, Henry's appreciation for beautiful women may be more helpful than you think. If he likes you, he'll arrange a tour of the residence."

"And wandering around his house will be helpful how?" Jesse asked.

Evie shot him a sharp look. His lips pressed into a thin line but he made a visible attempt to relax.

"It will be helpful because if you have access to the parts of the residence most visitors don't get to see over the course of the party, you will likely learn things about the high-ranking visitors that you wouldn't discover otherwise. At parties such as these, there is the ballroom, where most of the visitors gather. And there is the drawing room, where the upper echelon of government and society gather during the party to avoid the hoi polloi."

"I'm not sure we actually want to run into Secretary Gamble." Jesse's tone was carefully neutral.

"You're unlikely to be introduced," Darcy said.

"Then what's good about access to the drawing room?" Evie asked.

"The drawing room is like Las Vegas," Darcy said with a wry smile. "What happens there—"

"Stays there?" Evie finished.

"You'll hear things you won't hear otherwise if you're given access to the drawing room. If Henry takes you there himself, no one will question either your right to be there or your discretion." He looked at Jesse. "But there may be an issue."

"What's that?" Jesse asked, his voice tinged with suspicion.

"I don't know that Ms. Marsh's charms will extend to you."

Jesse's eyes narrowed. "Meaning?"

"He's not sure he can get an invitation for you to the drawing room." Evie looked at Jesse, bracing herself for his reaction.

He did not disappoint. "No way in hell."

"Do you want access to inside information or not?" Darcy asked.

"I'm her bodyguard. She doesn't go anywhere without me."

"I'm a DSS agent. Guarding people is my job."

"So you get to go to the drawing room with her."

"Of course," Darcy answered sensibly. "I'm Henry's godson."

"I don't know you from Adam's house cat—"

Darcy pulled his cell phone from the inner pocket of his tuxedo jacket and held it out to Jesse. "Call Maddox Heller. He knows me well. Ask him if I can be trusted to protect Ms. Marsh."

Jesse shook his head. "What am I supposed to be doing while you spirit my date away?"

Evie slanted a look at him. His date?

"There are things to learn among the unwashed, as well," Darcy said with a sly smile. "I suggest charming the women with your quaint accent. I hear women like a hillbilly drawl."

Evie closed her hand over Jesse's arm, feeling his muscles bunch beneath the fabric of his tux. "I won't stay in the drawing room all night," she said firmly, shooting a warning look at Darcy. "But if I get the chance, I have to go."

Jesse's eyes met hers and softened. "I know. But if you can charm old Henry into including me in the invitation to roam—"

"I can tell him you're a well-known security mogul," Darcy suggested, his voice bone-dry.

Evie shot the DSS agent a glare. "What is your problem?"

Darcy's eyebrows rose.

"Too much testosterone in a confined space." A hint of a smile touched the corner of Jesse's lips.

"Two males prowling about the same territory."

She darted a quick look from one man to the other. Territory? What territory? Were they talking about her?

Well. That would be something new. She was used to Rita being the object of desire, the prize to be won. Evie might as well have been invisible, for all the attention she'd ever attracted.

She'd never had two men vying for her attention before, if that was indeed what was going on. As stressful as it was turning out to be, she couldn't say she hated it.

The limousine pulled through a pair of iron gates and swept around the drive, under a short, square tunnel and into an interior courtyard where other cars and limousines lined up to decant their occupants.

When their limo reached the entrance, Darcy stepped from the vehicle and reached back inside to help Evie out. Jesse followed closely, his hand settling against the small of her back as they walked with Darcy up the weathered stone steps to the entry. A man with an earpiece met them at the door, speaking briefly with Darcy.

Evie eyed the opulence of the front entry, the pale stone walls and the tall glass-paned doors.

"The main hall is up those stairs," Darcy told them, nodding toward a sweeping set of stairs leading up to a second-floor landing. He led them upward, smiling broadly at the tall, red-cheeked man who stood on the landing, a stately woman with silver hair and warm green eyes by his side.

"Sir Henry!" Darcy shook the ambassador's hand. "Eleanor, you look smashing." He bent and kissed the woman's cheek. "I'm delighted to introduce my dear friends Evelyn Martin and her employer, Jesse Cooper." He bent closer to Henry, lowering his voice. "You may have heard of

Cooper Security? I believe you met his brother Richard some years ago when you were stationed in Burma."

Jesse's fingers flattened against Evie's back. She glanced up at him and saw him staring at Darcy, his eyes narrowed.

"Rick Cooper? Yes, yes! I remember him quite well. Handsome chap and excellent to have on your side in a tight spot." Ambassador Henry Steed shook Jesse's hand with enthusiasm. "I believe he was employed with Jackson Melville at MacLear at the time, was he not?"

"I believe so," Jesse answered carefully.

"Dreadful what happened to that company." The ambassador shook his head. "I hope your brother suffered no permanent ill effects from his association with MacLear."

"He works for me now," Jesse answered. "I'll be certain to give him your regards."

"Do! I would love to hear from him again. You must have him tell you about our adventure in Mandalay." The ambassador turned to Evie. "And it is a great delight to meet you, Ms. Martin. You look stunning."

Evie smiled. "Thank you, sir. What a beautiful home!"

"I wish I could claim credit for it, but it was here, as you see it, long before I arrived. Come, meet my wife, Eleanor."

After Jesse and Evie greeted the ambassador's

wife, Darcy pulled the ambassador aside briefly while Eleanor Steed answered some of Evie's questions about the architecture. A moment later, Darcy rejoined them, directing them down a long hallway with a harlequin-patterned marble-and-slate floor and into an enormous, ornate ballroom lined with faux Siena marble columns.

Evie had never attended a party at the British Embassy, but she'd been to enough tony Washington parties to be able to walk around the splendid ballroom without gaping at the massive chandeliers, the ornate carved plaster frieze lining the top of the walls or the striking Andy Warhol portrait of Queen Elizabeth hanging over the large mantel.

"I didn't know what to expect," she admitted, "but this is very—"

"Excessive?" Jesse drawled.

She cut her eyes at him. "Overwhelming."

"Well, get over that feeling, and quickly," Darcy said. "I was able to procure a tour of the house for both of you, and an invitation to visit the drawing room."

"Both of us?" Jesse looked surprised.

"Yes, both. I assume you know how to behave in good company."

The look Jesse gave Darcy would have killed a lesser man. Darcy merely answered with a placid smile.

"I hope you didn't mind my earlier name-dropping. I thought the ambassador's fortuitous prior connection to your brother, however tenuous, might help bring you into his inner circle more quickly."

"How did you know about it?" Jesse asked. "I didn't know my brother and the ambassador had ever met."

"After you contacted me and dropped Maddox Heller's name, I did my homework. In case Heller's time away from the Marines had dulled his normal instincts for trouble."

Evie slipped her hand into the crook of Jesse's arm, hoping to steer both men away from trouble before things got any tenser between them. "I don't see anyone here who'd recognize me," she said with relief.

Her days of attending parties with her father had ended almost a decade earlier, when she'd been skinny and shy, a gangly teenager still trying to get comfortable in her own skin. She'd eschewed makeup and worn her dark hair in a long braid down her back.

Even if someone she recognized had been here at the party, it was unlikely that person would look at the redhead in the blue chiffon dress and connect her to the awkward child she'd been ten years ago.

"What happens next?" Jesse placed his hand over Evie's where it lay in the crook of his arm.

Darcy's dark eyes scanned the ballroom. "I'll introduce the two of you to some people who will probably be in the drawing room later, after dinner. That way, you won't be so isolated when you go there."

"Won't you be there?" Evie asked.

"I have somewhere else to be," he said cryptically. "I'll try to join you there before the party ends." He nodded toward a group of men standing in the corner of the ballroom near one of the tall mirrors. "Come, let me introduce you to someone."

Evie and Jesse exchanged glances as they followed Darcy across the room. So the DSS agent had his own reason for being at the party. Maybe the secretary of energy wasn't the only potential bad guy who'd be at the ambassador's dinner that evening.

In short order, Darcy introduced them to a half-dozen fellow guests, including a brigadier general in the Air Force who recognized Jesse's name from the recent news about General Harlowe's kidnapping and subsequent release. He seemed inclined to ask Jesse questions about the case, but Jesse handled the inquiries with polite nonanswers that the general soon read—correctly—as well-mannered versions of "no comment."

They also met a talkative guest named Talbot Dreier, a pretty blonde in her mid-thirties whose husband, Robert, worked at the Department of Energy. "He's pretty low down the totem pole," she told Evie with a smile, edging away from the men, who had entered a discussion of college football.

Evie followed. "Everyone starts somewhere."

Talbot took a canapé from one of the white-suited butlers carrying trays of hors d'oeuvres. Evie selected a prosciutto-wrapped date and nibbled at it as she and Talbot went with the flow of partygoers out of the ballroom and across the corridor to the terrace overlooking the gardens.

"Stunning, isn't it?" Talbot asked, waving her half-eaten canapé at the symmetrical garden spreading out before them. "I wish you could have visited a few months ago when the roses were at their best."

"So you've visited here before?"

"A few times. Robert has become a particular favorite of Secretary Gamble, so when he has a chance to bring someone along to one of these events, Richard is often his choice."

"You've met the secretary yourself, then?"

"Of course. A charming man."

Evie heard an odd note in Talbot's otherwise cheerful voice. "He comes across very polished and urbane on television."

"Polished and urbane. Yes, that fits him well." Talbot snagged a champagne flute from a passing butler and lifted the glass in a brief salute. "To Secretary Gamble and his saint of a wife."

Now Evie knew there was more behind Talbot's words than their surface meanings. Clearly, she didn't have a completely positive opinion of Morris Gamble.

Evie dug a little deeper. "I didn't realize the secretary was married, although I shouldn't be surprised, should I? Behind every powerful man lurks at least one woman who made him what he is."

"At least one," Talbot agreed. "Or more than one."

"Theirs is a second marriage?"

Talbot's cherry-red lips curved in a wry smile. "Oh, no. Phyllis is his only wife. High school sweethearts." She took a sip of the champagne. When she spoke again, her voice was as dry as the wine. "Married nearly thirty years now."

Evie spotted Jesse watching her from the other side of the terrace. Even from that distance, she felt his gaze as surely as if he'd reached out and touched her. Dragging her gaze away from his, she smiled at Talbot, pretending to take her comments at face value. "What a romantic story."

"I'm not sure *romantic* is the right word." Talbot emptied her glass of champagne as a butler approached. She set the empty flute on the tray, snagging another. After another long sip of the sparkling wine, she leaned a little closer to Evie. "Men his age feel they still have a lot to prove. Don't you find that to be so?"

Evie widened her eyes. "He hasn't tried anything with you, has he?"

Talbot gave a little huff of surprised laughter. "No, no, definitely not me. I'm nowhere near important enough for the secretary to notice."

"So I suppose he's not bothering the clerical help,

then." Evie darted another quick glance across the terrace. Jesse had moved out of sight.

She swallowed a sigh.

"Oh, no. Unless you're already occupying the Oval Office, if you're serious about furthering your career, you never cheat down. You only cheat up." Talbot laughed at her own joke, her cheeks flushed from the champagne. "This town makes you cynical quickly."

Evie saw Talbot's gaze wander across the terrace to a spot near the door where a handsome man in his late thirties was talking to a well-dressed woman in her mid-forties. "Your husband?" she asked Talbot.

Talbot smiled, but Evie wasn't sure there was any pleasure behind the expression. "Yes, that's Robert."

"The woman he's talking to looks familiar."

"That's Senator Dalloway from West Virginia. She's probably lobbying him for fewer coal-industry regulations or something."

"Shouldn't she be talking to Secretary Gamble instead?"

"Good luck finding him." Talbot drained her second glass of champagne. "He came without Phyllis tonight, so he won't be sticking around long."

"Can't stand to stay away from her very long?"

Talbot laughed. "More like, it's his chance to disappear for a few hours without his wife wondering where he is." She started to trade her empty glass for another full one but held herself in check. She shot Evie an apologetic look. "I've been rambling, haven't I? I should know better than to drink on an empty stomach." She waved at one of the butlers carrying hors d'oeuvres. He detoured to her side and she selected a couple of tiny puff pastries from his tray, thanking him.

"I've enjoyed talking to you," Evie said, meaning it. And not just because the woman had provided a whole new element to Morris Gamble's connection to the Espera Group.

Talbot changed the topic to fashion, a subject that left Evie floundering for something intelligent to say. As soon as she could do so politely, she excused herself and went looking for Jesse. The look of relief in his eyes when he spotted her made her insides go liquid and warm.

"Don't wander off without letting me know," he said in a raspy growl.

"Sorry. Talbot was in the mood to talk, so I didn't want to interrupt." She tucked her hand in the crook of his arm and edged him away from the crowd, looking for someplace relatively quiet. She found an unoccupied corner of the ballroom and drew him with her into its cozy confines.

He looked at her, curious. "You learned something?"

"Maybe." She lowered her voice. "I think Secretary Gamble is having an affair."

Chapter Nine

Dinner, followed by a visit to the drawing room, interrupted Evie's account of her conversation with Talbot Dreier, forcing Jesse to chafe through an hour of polite conversation before he could even think about getting her alone again.

He saw his chance about thirty minutes into their visit to the drawing room, when the ambassador mentioned there would be dancing in the ballroom beginning at nine-thirty. Most of the ambassador's contemporaries, who made up the bulk of the drawing room crowd, chuckled at the announcement, but a few minutes later, the ambassador himself approached Jesse and Evie, smiling indulgently.

"We old grumps may prefer to stay here, smoke cigars and drink brandy, but you, my dear, are entirely too lovely to rub elbows with old men when the opportunity to dance with your companion presents itself." He looked at Jesse with an indulgent smile. "Go enjoy yourselves. You'll be staid and boring in due time."

Since the secretary of energy had already left for the evening, Jesse saw no reason not to do as the ambassador asked. The idea of dancing cheek to cheek with Evie posed a temptation he was in no mood to ignore tonight.

They made their way back to the ballroom, where a group of musicians had assembled in one corner of the room and was playing a slow, bluesy version of "I Only Have Eyes for You."

Evie looked up at Jesse. "The terrace?"

He nodded agreement, stifling an unexpected twinge of disappointment at being denied the chance to take her in his arms and dance her around the ballroom floor. But when they reached the terrace, he saw that most of the couples braving the cool night air were dancing as well, as the music from the ballroom carried all the way across the corridor to the outdoors.

Jesse held out his hand. "No avoiding it now."

She smiled and took his hand, letting him pull her into his arms. "I hope you're better at this than I am."

"I've been to a Marine Ball or two." He guided her slowly around the terrace, looking for a place where they could continue their conversation without being overheard. They headed down a set of steps into the garden itself before they found a spot secluded enough to risk speaking freely, and even then, they were in view of several other couples strolling through the gardens under the watchful eyes of embassy staff.

Jesse pulled her back into his arms and started to dance again, even though the music was barely audible from where they stood. "Loosen up, Evie. We have to look as if we're enjoying ourselves. Now, tell me what Talbot Dreier told you." Jesse bent his head closer, his cheek brushing hers. He closed his eyes for a second, fighting a fierce rush of desire that threatened to overwhelm his usual sense of control.

"It was all innuendo," Evie admitted, "but I don't think I'm wrong about what she meant." She repeated the conversation in detail. "Do you see why I think he's having an affair?"

He did. "Secretary Gamble was here for a few minutes early in the evening, gave his regrets to the ambassador and left."

"Did anyone else leave at the same time?" she asked, sounding curious.

"If so, nobody commented on it."

"Surely someone knows who he's seeing on the side, don't you think?" As a couple of guests moved near them, she stepped closer, lifting her face toward his. "Just pretend we're any young couple, dancing together in the British ambassador's rose garden." He heard a hint of dry humor in her voice.

If she knew what her touch did to him, would she find the situation so amusing? He could barely breathe, his heart racing like a rabbit chased by a coyote. Desire coiled low in his belly, a wily serpent preparing to strike.

He wanted her. Time to deal with reality.

He had never thought of her as anything but Rita's sister before now. Never considered what it would be like to touch her, kiss her or make love to her. He'd been Rita's fiancé and she'd been Rita's sister. The relationship had begun and ended there.

But he wasn't Rita's now. Rita had found someone else, someone she loved. And the way he felt these days when Evie was around—what if that meant something important? What if there could be more than simple animal attraction between them? Was that even possible?

She smelled good. Felt good, her curvy body soft against his.

She lifted her face, gazing at him. He saw a question there, deep in the smoldering blue depths of her eyes. His body quickening in answer, he tightened his arm around her waist, drawing her closer still. Her hands flattened against his back, her hips sliding against his thighs. He flexed his leg, and her body shifted, her legs parting, tangling with his.

He exhaled in a rush, pressing his forehead against hers. "Evie—"

She cradled his face between her palms. "Yes?"

He gazed at her, drowning in arousal.

Sliding upward, her breasts flattening against his chest, she kissed him.

A low groan rumbled through him as he responded, his mouth hard and hungry over hers. She parted her lips, inviting him in, her tongue dancing against his, sending shudders rippling down his spine. The sound of murmured conversation around them faded away, leaving only the thunderous cadence of his pulse in his ears and the ragged whisper of their mingled breaths.

You broke her heart.

General Marsh's voice rang in Jesse's head, a memory and an indictment. Another memory flashed through his desire-addled brain, breaking through the heat. Rita's face, stained by tears and misery. She'd asked so little of him, hadn't she? Just to find another career, away from the Marine Corps and the constant threat of danger. He could have done it. Hell, he had done it, when leaving the Marine Corps had suited his own needs.

He closed his hands over Evie's arms and set her away from him.

"No." He released his grip on her, feeling ill.

She stared at him, trying to breathe without gasping. "No?"

"We can't do this."

A look of dismay flitted across her face before her expression went neutral. "Oh."

He lifted his hand to touch her again but let it drop back to his side. "It's a bad idea on every level. I never should have let it happen. You're Rita's sister."

"Right." Her jaw tightened. "I'm sorry."

"It's not your fault. It's mine."

"Nobody's fault. And no harm done."

He narrowed his eyes. "Are you sure?"

"I got caught up in the romance of this place, I guess." She laughed lightly. "We're lucky it wasn't poor Agent Darcy who was out here dancing with me! What would he have thought when I planted one on him?"

Jesse felt a stab of jealousy at the thought, but he fought to cover it. "Right. Caught up in the moment."

"We should probably be mingling with the crowd, shouldn't we?" Around them, the other couples had started moving inside as the October night deepened, bringing with it an uncomfortable chill. He slowly followed Evie to the terrace doors.

EVIE WAS RELIEVED to run into Darcy back in the ballroom, glad for a buffer between her and Jesse after the fiasco in the garden. Darcy stood near the entrance, talking to a man Evie recognized as the State Department spokesman. She'd seen him on television a few times, although she couldn't remember his name.

Darcy introduced them. "Tom, this is an old friend of mine, Jesse Cooper, and his friend Evelyn Martin. Jesse, Evelyn, this is Tom Claiborne."

"Cooper," Claiborne said with a slight narrowing of his eyes. Evie felt Jesse go tense beside her. "The security expert."

"And you're the State Department spokesman," Jesse replied lightly, although Evie read wariness in his dark eyes.

Claiborne lowered his voice. "Your run-ins with Barton Reid were an anomaly. Reid is not representative of the entire Department of State."

"Right." Jesse didn't sound convinced.

Claiborne ignored his skepticism. "What are you doing in the capital?"

"Sightseeing. Been a while since I was in D.C. and I thought it was time to visit again."

"And scored a ticket to this party?" Claiborne arched his eyebrows.

"That was my doing," Darcy said smoothly. "I know Cooper through a mutual friend who asked me to make sure he got to meet Henry Steed, because they have a few things in common."

"Really?" It was Claiborne's turn to look skeptical.

"We're both avid anglers," Jesse said with a relaxed smile. "Although neither of us gets to indulge ourselves much these days. Too busy."

Claiborne turned his gaze to Evie. His scrutiny was sudden and intense, making her feel as if someone had turned a spotlight on her. "Forgive me, Ms. Martin. Rude of us to leave you out of the conversation."

She smiled, digging deep for control to keep from showing her unease. "I didn't feel left out," she assured him. "I've enjoyed watching your press briefings. You're very good at your job."

"Thank you."

If she'd hoped her polite but impersonal flattery would appease his interest and shift his focus away from her, she was disappointed. He snagged a glass of champagne as a butler passed and offered a glass to Evie.

"Thank you, no," she said with another polite smile. "I've had enough."

"You look so familiar," Claiborne said.

A lightning bolt of panic raced through her, but she struggled not to show any reaction. "I get that a lot. I must look like some actress or something."

"No, that's not it—"

"I'm sure you'll remember tomorrow, but for tonight, we must bid you good-night." Darcy stepped between Evie and Claiborne, clapping the State Department spokesman on the shoulder.

"So early?"

"I have a meeting first thing in the morning, and Jesse and Evelyn wanted to get an early start on their sightseeing in the morning." He turned to Evie and Jesse, a look of apology on his face. "Come, shall we bid Henry and Eleanor good-night?"

Jesse and Evie said a quick goodbye to Claiborne and followed Darcy from the ballroom. Moments later, they found Henry Steed and his wife in the drawing room.

"So soon?" Henry asked when Darcy told him they were leaving.

"I have a planning meeting in the morning for a state visit from a foreign dignitary," Darcy explained.

"And we're going to try to get in as much sightseeing tomorrow as possible," Jesse added, stealing Darcy's earlier excuse for them. "Evelyn hasn't visited D.C. before, and I don't want her to miss anything."

"My dear, do wear comfortable shoes!" Henry said with a soft laugh, shaking Evie's hand. "And take plenty of photographs. You will regret it if you don't."

Finally back in the limousine, Evie slumped against the seat back, feeling boneless. "I think Claiborne recognized me. It's just a matter of time before he figures it out."

"How would he know you?" Jesse asked.

"Her photograph has been all over the local papers," Darcy said. "She looks different now, of course," he said, waving his hand at her short, dyed hair, "but—"

"But maybe not different enough," Jesse finished for him. He looked at Evie. "We'd better not go back to the motel. Too many eyes around there. Too many people who might figure out who you really are." He shook his head. "I shouldn't have brought you here with me."

She raised her eyebrows. "Let's not go through this again."

"I can check you out of the motel if you wish," Darcy suggested. "And arrange new lodgings."

"Any other motel we check into will pose the same problem," Evie said. "Unless you're suggesting we leave D.C. altogether."

"Maybe we should." Jesse's gaze darkened.

"No. We finally have a lead, as nebulous as it is—"

"A lead?" Darcy asked.

Evie and Jesse both looked at the DSS agent, then back at each other.

"Or is this a need-to-know situation?" Darcy asked.

"He might know something that could help us," Evie said softly.

Jesse frowned.

"I realize you have reason not to trust people in general at the moment." Darcy's tone was quiet and calm. "But I *am* on your side. I have seen the damage done by MacLear and the Special Services Unit. I've lost friends and colleagues to their underhanded machinations. If what you're doing now will bring them down for good, I will do whatever I can to give you aid. But I am hamstrung if you keep vital information from me."

"Tell him," Evie urged.

Jesse took a deep breath, glancing toward the limousine chauffeur barely visible through the smoky glass partition separating the passenger seats from the driver's seat. "Can he hear us?"

Darcy shook his head. "The glass is soundproof as well as bullet resistant. To speak to him, I have to press an intercom button."

"Could the limo be bugged?"

"Oh, for goodness' sake!" Evie turned to Darcy. "It's not a state secret or anything. We just think Secretary Gamble may be cheating on his wife." She summarized her conversation with Talbot Dreier, also pointing out the secretary of energy's impolitic quick exit from the party.

Darcy's only reaction was a slight twitch of one eyebrow. "Infidelity is hardly an anomaly in D.C. politics."

"Still, it gives us a lever," Jesse said. "If the Espera Group is corrupt enough to hire the SSU to do their dirty work, they have no business influencing global energy policy. We need to know just how involved Secretary Gamble might be in their push for the treaty and stop him."

"And you think knowing that he's cheating on his wife will give you the leverage you need to do that?" Darcy sounded skeptical.

"It's more than we had before today," Evie said.

"But what do you have, really?" Darcy gave a dismissive wave of his hand. "Innuendo at best, from a woman who believes politics and cronyism are keeping her husband from rising more quickly in the government ranks. She's hardly a disinterested observer."

Evie's exasperation level was reaching the boiling point. "So you agree with Jesse? We should just run back home to Alabama with our tails tucked between our legs?"

"I'm pretty sure I never suggested that," Jesse murmured drily.

"I think it's an opening. But just an opening. You need more."

"We're not stupid. We know that." Jesse's scornful look would have felled a lesser man, but Darcy merely looked placid and mildly amused.

"If we need more, we'll get more," Evie said firmly.

"Any ideas how you intend to do that?"

The limousine's arrival at the curb outside Annie Harlowe's apartment saved Evie from having to answer. Instead, she gave Darcy a polite nod as the driver came around to open the door from them.

"Thank you for the ride and the party invitation," she said primly, letting the driver help her out.

Darcy stepped out with them. "My offer to check you out of your previous motel stands. Do you know where you'll be staying?"

Jesse looked at Evie. "Why not here at Annie's apartment? Cooper Security is paying for the place anyway, and there are two bedrooms."

Evie felt a little chill dart down her neck. Two

bedrooms. *In other words, don't expect a continuation of the kiss in the garden.*

"Good idea." She dropped her gaze.

"Very well. I'll collect your things and bring them here in the morning. Do you have what you need for this evening?"

"I do," Evie answered. She could sleep in her underwear and the T-shirt she'd changed out of when she put on the borrowed dress. "What should we do about the dresses and tux?"

"I'll collect those from you when I bring you your things," Darcy offered. "I have a way to get in touch with Quinn, and he'll handle it from there. I'll be in touch."

Jesse laid his hand on the small of Evie's back, guiding her toward the apartment building's entrance as Darcy closed the limo door behind him and the long black car pulled away from the curb. "Long night, huh?"

"Yes," she answered, wishing he wouldn't touch her. Even though she knew the light brush of his hand on her back meant nothing to him, it was a visceral reminder of her own unattainable desires. Kissing him tonight had been a mistake of massive proportions, if for no other reason than how it had shown her exactly what she was missing.

A ten-year crush on her sister's ex-fiancé had never been anything more than a pleasant dream, an idle what-if. She'd never really let those girlish feelings interfere with the other relationships she'd had since she was seventeen. She'd had a serious relationship in college, even considering marriage before the romance had fallen apart. Since college, she'd dated several men without letting Jesse Cooper's memory get in the way.

But now that she knew what it was like to kiss him, knew how his touch made her blood sing, how could she ever pretend she wanted anyone else?

Chapter Ten

"Is that him?" Evie looked over the rim of her coffee cup toward the Department of Energy building. Her short hair was tucked up under a baseball cap she'd borrowed from Jesse, and a pair of sunglasses hid her bright blue eyes. She'd been spooked by what Tom Claiborne had said to her the night before about looking familiar, so she'd taken pains to disguise herself behind loose clothes and the cap and glasses. She seemed satisfied she looked nondescript.

What she really looked was damned adorable. Jesse was having trouble paying attention to the side exit, where Secretary Gamble should be appearing anytime now.

"No, not him," he said, dragging his gaze from her pert profile long enough to check out the suit-clad man she pointed out.

"What if he takes a car?"

"Darcy said he leaves the building on foot every Wednesday around lunchtime."

"And you trust Darcy now?" She turned her face toward him, but with her eyes hidden behind the glasses, he found he couldn't read her expression.

He quelled the urge to remove the sunglasses. "I don't trust anyone in this bloody town but you. But we can't afford to ignore leads when they fall in our laps."

"Unless this is a trap."

"Darcy knows where we were last night. If he wanted to entrap us, he could have just made a phone call and had the FBI waiting on our doorstep."

"So, not a trap. A wild-goose chase."

"This whole trip has been a wild-goose chase." He shrugged. "So what's new?"

Evie's lips tightened. She looked back toward the side exit and sat up straighter. "That's definitely him."

Following her gaze, Jesse felt a jolt of adrenaline rush through him as he recognized Morris Gamble's silver hair and patrician profile. "He's coming this way. Wait him out."

There were no staffers with Gamble, Jesse noted as the secretary walked at an energetic clip toward the concrete bench where he and Evie sat. The secretary didn't spare either of them a look as he passed and turned left, heading down Independence Avenue toward the Metro station.

"Wait," Jesse reiterated as he felt Evie's body twitch beside him.

"We're going to lose him."

"No, we're not." He stood and tossed the remains of his coffee in a nearby trash bin. Evie did the same, falling into step as they followed the secretary from a distance of thirty yards behind.

"He's turning into the Metro station," Evie murmured as Gamble headed for the train station a couple of blocks later. They caught up, walking into the station about ten yards behind him. They had already loaded fare cards with enough money to get them anywhere they wanted to go for the next couple of days, so they didn't have to stop before they reached the turnstiles.

Gamble boarded a Blue Line train heading toward the L'Enfant Plaza transfer station, avoiding the mass of commuters huddling near the center of the train by boarding near the back. Jesse and Evie followed, taking seats a couple of rows behind the secretary.

If anyone else on the train recognized the secretary of energy, they showed no signs of it. He wasn't the most recognizable of the president's cabinet, Jesse supposed. Maybe that's why Gamble chose this form of travel rather than a private car—nobody would even notice him amid the throng of federal workers who filled the trains every weekday.

"Any idea where he's going?" Evie murmured.

Jesse shook his head, beginning to worry that she might be right. Maybe they *were* on a wild-goose chase. Darcy claimed to be on their side, but he worked for an offshoot of the State Department, the same government department that had produced a corrupt bastard like Barton Reid, who'd left a trail of dead bodies and ruined lives in his wake.

"He could be going to meet his girlfriend," Evie suggested.

"I hope that's not all it is." Jesse fidgeted with his fare card. If they were simply following Gamble to a romantic rendezvous—

"I think we're at the transfer station," Evie said quietly. The train slowed as they pulled into the L'Enfant Plaza station. Gamble stood as the train stopped, and fell into the line of passengers preparing to disembark.

Jesse caught Evie's hand, tugging her with him through the crowd. They had to move at a clip to keep from losing Gamble in the roiling sea of humanity filling the platform outside the train.

After a heart-stopping couple of seconds, he caught sight of the secretary again, walking briskly toward the Green Line train heading south. "There," he told Evie, pulling her with him as he hurried to catch up.

Gamble boarded a train headed south toward the Navy Yard and the Anacostia River. Jesse didn't know enough about the D.C. area to know if his choice of destinations was odd, but Evie gave a low murmur of surprise when she saw the train they were boarding.

"Something wrong?" he asked as they settled a few rows behind Gamble.

"We're heading across the Anacostia River."

"What does that mean?"

"That's not the wealthiest part of D.C. Mostly residential and urban."

"Not the usual hangout for a presidential cabinet member, you mean."

"Not exactly where I'd choose to have a romantic assignation," she said flatly. "Not when there are any number of luxury hotels not two miles from where he works."

"But if he doesn't want to be seen—"

"If he cared about being seen, why would he take the Metro instead of a private car?" she asked, echoing his earlier thought.

"Then maybe *she* doesn't want to be seen."

Evie slanted a look at him. He felt a rippling sensation shoot through his gut to land low in his belly, a potent reminder of just how vulnerable he was becoming where Evie was concerned.

Don't think about the kiss, a desperate voice whispered in his head.

Unfortunately, it seemed to be all he could think about. The memory of those stolen moments in the rose garden haunted him, making him wonder what might have happened if he hadn't stopped her.

"What if his lover is someone well-known?" he asked quietly, struggling to put all thoughts of her soft, tempting lips out of his mind.

"Interesting question," she murmured. "Talbot did say men in politics always cheat up."

The train stopped twice before they pulled into the Anacostia station. Jesse watched Gamble carefully, in case he moved at the last moment and put them at a disadvantage. But he remained seated all the way, even after the train had swapped out passengers at the Anacostia station.

Next stop, Congress Heights.

"What's in Congress Heights?" he asked Evie, keeping his voice low.

"Mostly apartments and homes. The Barry Farm neighborhood. A few shopping centers." She peered out the window as lights on the track began to flash, warning that they were nearing the station. "There's a psychiatric hospital there, too. St. Elizabeth's."

The name tugged lightly at the back of his mind, but he didn't have time to ponder its meaning, for as the train pulled into the Congress Heights Metro station, Morris Gamble rose from his seat and moved briskly to the exit door.

Jesse rose as well, catching Evie's hand and tugging her to her feet. Swept up in the throng crowding the central platform, they struggled to keep Gamble in view. Jesse lost sight of the secretary as they reached the escalators. "Damn it, I can't see him."

The escalators deposited them at street level and the tightly packed crowd spread out, exiting the pavilion-like shelter into the bright midday sun.

Evie shaded her eyes. "Do you see him?"

Jesse scanned the flat, concrete square. "There!" He nodded toward the bus shelter near the curb. Gamble was striding purposefully past the gathering crowd waiting for the next bus, heading for the crosswalk.

Jesse and Evie hurried to catch up before the light turned, putting them closer to the secretary than Jesse liked. "Hold back a little once we reach the other side," he murmured to Evie as they stepped quickly to beat the light. "Don't want to spook him."

They slowed their pace once they reached the sidewalk, letting Gamble put some distance between them. "Where is he going?" Evie asked.

Not to St. Elizabeth's hospital, Jesse thought, as the secretary walked past the wide entrance to the tree-lined campus and continued down Alabama Avenue into a residential neighborhood, slowing only when he neared a pair of men standing at the next corner.

Jesse caught Evie's hand, instantly on alert as one of the men turned to greet the secretary.

They were the two men who'd kidnapped Evie from the wedding.

One of them spotted Jesse and Evie. He stared, his expression betraying surprise. It was a split second of warning, but Jesse took advantage of it, tightening his grip on Evie's hand and darting across the nearest lawn.

Hand in hand, they raced down the cross street

for half a block until Evie tugged him toward a narrow ally that cut behind the houses on that block. The pavement in the alley was uneven, the cracks sprouting weeds that caught their shoes as they ran, threatening to send them sprawling. Behind them, the pounding of footsteps on the pavement seemed to thunder down the narrow lane. Jesse didn't waste time looking back, but apparently Evie did, for her grip on his hand tightened and she put on a new burst of speed.

They reached the next street and dashed across, dodging a car and nearly barreling into a trio of garbage cans that stood near the entrance of the next alley. Something exploded very close to Jesse's right ear, splintering the wood of the shed they were passing. He knew that muted blatting sound, knew the effects of a bullet slamming into a wood frame.

"They're shooting at us!" Evie rasped.

They needed to get out of the alley, but most of the yards along the lane were fenced in, blocking easy escape routes. The mouth of the alley loomed ever closer, and Jesse took a chance, zigzagging across the uneven pavement, his focus entirely on the cross street ahead.

They burst from the alley and paused only long enough to look left and right, seeking the closest route of escape. Jesse tugged Evie's hand and turned right, ignoring the growing burn in his legs as he heard another flat bark of a sound-suppressed pistol in the alley behind them.

She kept up, her shorter legs churning that much harder to match his longer strides. Despite his desperation to get her to safety, Jesse spared a moment of admiration for her courage and pluck.

A large thoroughfare loomed ahead of them, the crossing light already blinking a warning. Jesse took a chance anyway, pounding relentlessly toward the other side of the road.

The traffic light turned red as they neared the sidewalk, car horns blaring at their folly. Jesse tugged Evie behind him the last few feet and hit the sidewalk running.

A squeal of tires behind them followed by a harsh thudding sound and shouts of horror broke through the haze of panic driving Jesse relentlessly forward. He faltered to a halt, slowed by the tug of Evie's hand as she came to a stop, as well.

Behind them lay a horrific scene. A car sprawled almost sideways a few feet past the crosswalk, the young female driver emerging from her open door, shaking and crying. Traffic on both sides of the street had screeched to a halt, and both drivers and pedestrians were beginning to stream into the street, gathering around two bloody bodies sprawled in the street several feet beyond the crosswalk.

The men who had been chasing them had stepped into the crosswalk a few seconds too late, running straight into traffic.

Movement across the street caught Jesse's attention. Morris Gamble walked slowly toward the edge of the crosswalk, staring first at the mangled bodies of his companions, then across the tangle of onlookers to lock gazes with Jesse.

He stared at Jesse for a moment, expressionless. Then he slowly turned and walked away from the scene, disappearing back up the street.

"We have to get out of here," Jesse urged, tugging Evie's hand. With the other people on the street concentrating on the aftermath of the accident, they had a chance to simply blend into the crowd and make their getaway.

"Wait. One of them is still alive." Evie pulled her hand out of Jesse's and stepped into the street before he could stop her.

He hurried after her, watching the crowd around them for any sign that the two men who'd come after them might have accomplices in the area, but all he saw was genuine concern for the wounded men, along with an unsurprising dose of grim curiosity.

People were already on their phones, probably talking to 9-1-1, which meant the Metro police would be here soon. He and Evie needed to be far away from the scene before that happened.

"Evie—"

She had already pulled close to the injured man, edging through the onlookers to kneel next to him.

His injuries were grievous, Jesse saw, tamping down a rush of nausea. He'd seen his share of battlefield casualties, enough to know this man wasn't likely to live long enough to make it to the hospital. Despite the efforts of a man trying to stanch the flow of blood pouring from the man's half-severed leg, there wasn't much hope of stopping the bleeding. He'd clearly torn an artery and was bleeding out.

The man's eyes fluttered open suddenly, focusing with effort on Evie's face. Jesse watched, his heart in his throat, as the man reached for Evie's arm. He started forward, but an onlooker blocked him, and he could only watch, anxious and powerless, as Evie bent toward the dying man.

"He's saying something," one of the onlookers murmured.

Jesse pushed to the edge of the crowd in time to see the man's hand fall away from Evie's arm. She rose, her gaze scanning the crowd until it locked with Jesse's. She stared at him for a mute, pained moment and started walking away, leaving him to catch up with her.

"What did he say?" one of the onlookers asked the man who had redoubled his effort to stop the bleeding.

The man didn't answer.

Jesse hurried after Evie, who stopped near the clump of onlookers surrounding the body of the other accident victim. It was the man who'd been driving the Audiovisual Assets truck, Jesse knew, although his face was almost too bloody and mangled to recognize. Unlike his companion, this man hadn't survived the initial impact of the car. He'd been thrown twenty feet down the street and hit headfirst. There would be no last-minute efforts to save him. It was too late.

Evie turned to Jesse as he caught up with her. "I didn't want them to die. Even when they were shooting at us."

"I know." Wrapping his arm around her, he guided her out of the way of traffic. She melted into him, making it hard to walk, but he didn't care. He liked the feel of her body aligned with his, a warm and welcome reminder that they were both alive and unhurt.

He led her down the next street, growing alarmed as he felt her body begin to shudder. They began passing neighborhood residents drawn toward the accident scene by the wail of emergency-vehicle sirens, earning looks of curiosity as they went against the tide of foot traffic.

With no desire to pique anyone else's curiosity, Jesse looked for a quick exit, spotting the mouth of a narrow alley leading between two redbrick buildings. He guided her there, quickening his steps.

She pulled away suddenly, flattening her back against the hard brick side of one of the buildings closest to the alley. "He said 'Katrina.'"

Jesse stepped toward her, but she held up her hand, keeping him at a distance. She bent slightly at the waist, as if struggling for breath, and her voice, when it came again, sounded as if she were speaking from a great distance. "That's all he said, but he said it three times. His grip on my arm tightened. Just for a minute. Not much more strength than a baby's, but it tightened." She rubbed her wrist, tucking it close to her chest.

Jesse watched her struggle with emotion, his heart aching for her. He'd seen death many times during his missions with the Marine Corps. More times than he ever wanted to count again, although he'd had to account for each casualty when they'd happened, feeling the weight of them more and more the higher he'd climbed up the chain of command.

"It's not your fault," he said quietly. "You didn't make them run into traffic after you."

Her blue eyes lifted to meet his, red-rimmed and glittering with unspilled tears. "I know. But—"

"No buts." He stepped forward, pulling her into his arms. She didn't protest this time, melting into him again until he felt as if he'd absorbed her into himself. It was a disconcerting but strangely comforting sensation, her body pressed so liquidly to his, her heartbeat hammering into his chest as if it were his own.

"I should have gone to a safe house." Her voice rumbled through his chest, setting off a tremor low in his gut. "I should have done as you asked. I've only made things harder for you."

He threaded his fingers through her hair and

lifted her face, forcing her gaze up to meet his. "I wouldn't have found the connection to Gamble without you. And you're the one who ferreted out the affair—"

"And where has that gotten us? Katrina? It could mean anything."

"It's a step closer." He touched his forehead to hers.

Her hands tightened on the front of his T-shirt, her fingers curling in the fabric. The air between them supercharged, making his heart skip a beat.

She gazed up at him, the first tear spilling down her cheek in a slow trickle. Naked need burned in her eyes, striking sparks against the hard ache of desire squeezing like an iron fist in the center of his chest.

All the self-control drilled into Jesse by over a decade in the Marine Corps wasn't strong enough to resist the siren song of Evie's desperate gaze. Jesse bent his head to hers again, helpless against the force of his own desire.

He captured her mouth beneath his, staked a claim he knew he had no right to declare. And as her lips moved fiercely, hungrily against his own, all thoughts of right and wrong disappeared into a gulf of pure, all-consuming need.

Chapter Eleven

The first kiss with Jesse had been something of a revelation, betraying a tenderness behind the ramrod-straight backbone of a born Marine. The second kiss, however, served as a shattering reminder that for all his moments of gentleness, he possessed a core of hard, polished steel, powerful and unyielding.

She had no conscious memory of moving, but suddenly the rough brick of the building behind her was digging into her back, the tactile sensation registering only faintly, swamped by desire so primal, so elemental, that even the rasp of brick against her flesh felt like raw pleasure.

She had promised herself, after their first kiss, that she wouldn't let herself fall for the fantasy again. But her good intentions crumbled like a sand castle under the onslaught of Jesse Cooper's seduction.

He had big, strong hands, slightly rough in texture despite his recent months behind an office desk. As she melted into him, boneless with surrender, he moved his hands slowly over the curves of her shoulders and down her arms, tracing a trail of fire across her flesh.

The small, sane part of her brain that still functioned sounded warning bells when he dropped his hands to her waist and pulled her lower body flush with his. A growl of frustration rumbled in his throat, and she echoed the sound with a soft moan of need.

Jesse pulled back suddenly, letting her go so quickly that she had to plant her feet and press her back against the wall to keep from sliding to the ground.

"Katrina," he murmured, his brow furrowing.

She stared at him a moment, not understanding. Then she remembered the sound of the dying man's words, the rattle of blood in his throat and the look of desperation in his fading eyes.

Katrina, he'd moaned. She felt a sudden wave of nausea and bent forward, resting her hands on her knees.

Jesse laid his hand on her back. "Are you okay?"

She took a couple of deep breaths, her head clearing. The nausea settled down to a faint queasiness she thought she could bear. "Yeah. You had a thought about what that man meant?"

"I thought at first maybe it had something to do with the Gulf Coast hurricane by the same name, but that made no sense," he said, starting to pace a little as if he was still forming the thought in his head. "Anyway, it's kind of crazy, but something's been niggling at me since we figured out where Gamble was going, and it finally connected just a second ago. St. Elizabeth's."

Evie scraped her hair away from her flushed face, not following. "St. Elizabeth's?"

"This morning, before we left the apartment, I bought a newspaper from the stand downstairs. I thought maybe there'd be a story about the Espera Group or Gamble or something that could give us a little insight. There wasn't anything like that, but there was a profile of the president's chief of staff and her personal crusade to raise more funds for St. Elizabeth's Hospital. Seems she grew up in the Congress Heights neighborhood and her aunt, a nurse at St. Elizabeth's, still owns a home in the area—"

A lightbulb went on in Evie's head, too. "Oh, my God. The president's chief of staff is named Katrina Hilliard."

THEY MADE IT SAFELY BACK to the apartment without drawing any more attention to themselves, although there had been a scary moment during their walk back to the Congress Heights Metro station when they overheard a couple of police officers mention wanting to talk to a female witness who'd helped one of the dying men, then suddenly disappeared from the crowd.

"If they put out a description of you," Jesse had warned Evie on the train ride back to Annie Harlowe's Arlington apartment, "we may have to get out of D.C. sooner than we wanted."

She was in the bathroom now, while he was hunting through Annie's supply of canned goods to find something to tempt her into eating a late lunch. He had heard the water running earlier, but not the shower. Maybe she was taking a tub bath instead.

An image flickered through his mind—Evie slick and naked beneath a shimmery layer of frothy bubbles, gazing up at him with invitation in her eyes. A flood of heat settled low in his belly in response, and he kicked himself for letting his thoughts run so freely out of control.

They hadn't discussed the kiss in the alley, both of them clearly avoiding the topic in favor of less volatile subjects, like running for their lives. But if they planned to share this apartment much longer, Jesse knew they were going to have to talk seriously about boundaries.

As he searched the cabinets for more food choices, his cell phone rang. The untraceable phone he was using on this trip didn't have caller ID, so he couldn't know who was on the other end of the call without answering.

He let it ring two more times before he answered. "Yeah?"

"It's Megan," his sister said briskly. "You haven't

checked in since yesterday morning. The natives are getting restless around here."

"Sorry. We've been busy. We've had a hell of a day."

"Been a little rough here, too," Megan said flatly. "General Marsh dropped by the offices, demanding to know why the hell you'd taken his daughter with you when he'd clearly set things up so that you'd leave her behind in a safe place."

Jesse grimaced. "If I thought she'd have stayed put anywhere I stashed her, I would have, believe me. But she was really pissed off by the ambushes the day of the wedding, and she knew I was heading to D.C.—"

"So she planned to go to Washington with or without you," Megan finished for him. "She always was the more headstrong of the Marsh sisters."

Jesse's grimace curved into a smile. "Still is."

"I know you can't stay on the phone long. Anything you need to catch us up on?"

"Yeah, one or two things." He gave his sister a terse, bare-bones version of the past two days. "I don't know if the guy survived his injuries, but I really don't see how he could."

"Wow," Megan said after a brief silence. "A party at the British ambassador's home and a foot chase through the streets of southeast D.C. all in a forty-eight-hour period. And you call *us* trouble magnets."

Jesse heard the bathroom door open behind him.

"Meggie, I've got to go. Tell everyone we're fine, and tell the general Evie's safe and we'll catch him up on everything as soon as we can."

He hung up after a quick goodbye and turned to greet Evie. But she wasn't there. And her bedroom door was closed.

He set about heating up cans of turnip greens and pinto beans, wishing he had some corn bread to go with them. But he did find a pleasant surprise in one of the lower cabinets—a box of white-chocolate macadamia-nut cookies that hadn't been opened and hadn't yet reached their expiration date.

Evie had a sweet tooth. Always had, ever since he'd met her. When he'd first been pursuing Rita, he'd made Evie his conspirator, keeping her supplied with her favorite candy bars as payment for her efforts on his behalf.

He kept waiting for Evie to emerge from the bedroom to join him, so he could show her the closest thing they'd had to a home-cooked dinner in several days. But the bedroom door remained closed, and he heard nothing but silence from within.

He crossed to the door. "Evie?" he said quietly.

There was no answer from inside.

Fingers of unease prickled up his back. He tried the door handle, relieved to find it unlocked.

"Evie, I'm coming in to check on you." He eased the door open and looked inside. The room was dark, the curtains on the window near the bed closed to block out the late-afternoon light. It took a second for his eyes to adjust to the darkness enough to spot Evie curled up on the bed beneath a brown plaid flannel blanket. Her eyes were closed and he could hear her slow, even breathing.

He started to retreat, but a soft whimpering noise from the bed drew him back inside. He walked quietly to her bedside and crouched next to her, watching with concern as her forehead crinkled and her lips began to quiver.

Tears trickled from the corners of her eyes, spilling over her nose and cheeks to fall on the pillow. "No," she whispered, even that soft sound drowning in despair. "No, please—"

"Evie, sweetie." He touched her cheek, brushing away a tear. "Evie, wake up."

She stirred, her eyes fluttering open. She jerked to a sitting position, scrambling backward until her shoulders hit the headboard.

"It's just me, Evie. Jesse."

"Jesse." His name escaped from her throat in a soft hiss.

"You were dreaming."

She covered her face with her hands for a moment, letting them slide down and away. "Right."

"Was it about this afternoon?"

She shook her head. "It was weird. I don't really remember all the details, but someone was in my apartment. Back home. It was dark and I don't think I ever saw his face, but he was everywhere I turned."

Jesse eased down on the edge of the bed. "I imagine you're feeling pretty trapped. Stuck here with me, away from your family and friends." Now that his eyes had adjusted to the dim light, he could see her well enough to read the subtle shift in her expression.

She shook her head. "I don't feel trapped. I feel safe with you."

"I'm not sure I've given you reason to." He touched the back of her hand where it lay in her lap. "I've been waiting for you to bring up what happened in the alley. I mean, don't women usually want to analyze things like that? What they mean?"

"I'm not sure talking about it will answer any questions."

"Why's that?"

She looked at him, her gaze level and strong. "I'm Rita's sister, right?"

He'd said that, hadn't he? Used it as an excuse to put a stop to their kiss in the rose garden. "I'm not sure you and I mean the same thing by that—"

"Does it matter?" She shrugged. "There are plenty of other reasons to keep our hands to ourselves. I'm your employee, we're in a high-tension situation that's not exactly conducive to making smart decisions—"

"I hurt Rita. I didn't want to, but it happened. And you might be willing to overlook that enough to work for me, but I don't think you could ever put it behind us. I know your parents couldn't." He looked down at his hand, realized he was still holding hers and pulled his away. "I think I've hurt the Marsh family enough for one lifetime."

"Interesting that you assume you'll hurt me." There was no emotional inflection in her voice, only a hint of objective curiosity. He didn't like not being able to read what she was feeling. Evie was usually an open book to him, her heart in her bright blue eyes. Seeing her so closed off from him made his chest ache.

"I'm not a good bet where relationships are concerned. I'm stubborn and set in my ways, and I work in a high-stress, dangerous job."

"Right."

Her calm nonresponse annoyed him. "So you understand."

"Sure. I understand." She scooted off the bed, stretching her arms over her head. "Do I smell food?"

"Yes, you do. And I hope to hell it's not burning."

Fortunately, the beans and turnip greens weren't overcooked, and he spooned the vegetables onto a couple of plates Evie retrieved from the cupboard. "Sorry these weren't home-cooked," he said.

"They're not bad."

"But not as good as your mom's."

"Well, no. My mom grew up on a farm in Mississippi."

"I know."

She smiled at him again, driving away more of

his uneasiness. "Right. She made it her mission to teach me to cook. I wasn't the most willing of students—I preferred to be outside running and climbing and chasing boys away from my secret fort—but she was relentless."

"She taught me a few things, too." He answered her smile with one of his own. "One time she showed me how to make peanut-butter fudge. Shannon still asks for peanut-butter fudge as her Christmas present from me. Every year."

"I love my mom's peanut-butter fudge. Of course, I have a voracious sweet tooth."

"I know. I bribed you with enough candy bars." As she looked up at him, a hint of surprise in her blue eyes, he remembered the cookies. "And speaking of your sweet tooth…"

He crossed to the cabinet and pulled out the bag of cookies. He laid the bag on the table in front of her, grinning down at her. "You'll owe me a lot of favors for finding those for you, Marsh."

Her gaze snapped up to meet his. "You're good."

He laughed softly. "Save me one, okay?"

She pulled one of the cookies from the bag and gave it a slow, deep sniff, as if she were a wine taster about to sample a rare vintage. "Mmm, macadamia nuts."

"I was hoping you'd like them."

"What's not to like?" She took her first bite. A low moan of pleasure escaped her throat, shooting straight to his sex. He had to shift in his seat to relieve the sudden pressure in his jeans.

She finished that bite, waving the cookie at him. "What brought this on? What are you bribing me to do this time?"

"No bribe." His voice came out rough. He cleared his voice and continued. "I just thought you could use a home-cooked meal. Sort of."

"To take my mind off this afternoon."

"Yeah." He should probably stop there, but he didn't like the way their conversation in the bedroom had ended. "And I wanted to make you happy."

She stopped in the middle of taking another bite, her eyes meeting his over the cookie. "I'm not unhappy."

He wished he could believe her. She'd once been one of the happiest people he'd ever met, a smiling woman-child who could find the humor in any situation and the positive spin on the worst of situations.

He hadn't seen that person in a long time. Certainly not since she came to work at Cooper Security. She was energetic and smart, industrious and prone to taking the initiative, even quick with a smile and a kind word. But under it all, he'd caught glimpses of darkness, as if there was a piece of her soul, carefully hidden from view, that ached and bled.

Until she'd walked into the Cooper Security of-

fices looking for a job, he hadn't seen her in nearly
nine years. The child had grown up, lived up to
the promise and potential he'd seen in her handsome face and gangly limbs. Handsome had become beautiful, her angular figure softening into
well-proportioned curves. But something vital,
something he'd always remembered with fondness,
seemed to have fled.

"Evie, after Rita and I broke up—" The trill of
his cell phone interrupted him. With a flicker of
annoyance, he answered the phone. "Yeah?"

"Jesse, it's Shannon." His youngest sister sounded
distraught. "Something horrible has happened."

His gut clenched with dread. Was it one of the
family? Or someone in Evie's family? "What?"

"Someone broke into Lydia Ross's house while
she was there. She's in the hospital, and the doctors
don't know if she's ever going to wake up."

Chapter Twelve

"I want to hurt someone."

Jesse looked up from his laptop to find Evie sitting on the arm of the sofa, her fists clenched. Her eyes blazed with anger and, if he was reading her correctly, no small amount of fear.

"So do I," he admitted. "But there's not much we can do from here."

"Those bastards have killed people. Good people. Your brother-in-law, General Ross—"

Jesse crossed to her, catching her balled-up fists in his hands. He gently pried her fingers open, threading them through his own. "I know. And probably a lot more people we don't even know about."

"All for the sake of the Espera Group." Her brow creased. "The continued tensions in Kaziristan are their doing, aren't they?"

Jesse gave her hands a light squeeze. "Probably."

"And the U.S. has been wondering for years where El Cambio has been getting funds to keep up the fight against the government of Sanselmo, considering their group has lost the support of the people. What if it's been the Espera Group bank-rolling their terrorist attacks?"

"I think that's another strong possibility," Jesse agreed. Sanselmo, a small country on the northern coast of South America, had finally begun to make significant reforms in favor of economic and social freedoms after years of struggle. The country would have come farther faster without the incessant acts of violence perpetrated by El Cambio, a neo-Marxist terrorist group. "Sanselmo's oil reserves have barely been tapped at all. They could end up being a huge world exporter if they can keep El Cambio from sabotaging their oil rigs and refineries."

"Has the Espera Group been stirring up the ongoing troubles in the Middle East? Iran, Iraq, Afghanistan—"

"Probably."

She stared at him, looking frustrated. "How can you be so calm about it? I want to break things!"

He released one of her hands, holding on to the other as he led her back to the small desk where he'd been working at the laptop. "I've been channeling my anger into some research." He pulled up another chair for her and sat at the computer.

She leaned closer, reading the news article he'd pulled up on the internet. "Well, what do you know?

Katrina Hilliard is another fan of what the Espera Group has planned."

"We don't know that she's specifically supporting the Espera Group," he cautioned, settling in his own chair. "But she supports global control and regulation of oil production and sales, as well as a more equitable sharing of what she calls a 'planetary resource' belonging to all the people of Earth."

"It's easy to see why so many people buy into the idea without giving it more thought," Evie murmured. "It sounds so reasonable. Until you realize it trounces on the very notion of private property and national sovereignty."

"And it puts an unelected group of custodians in charge of massive amounts of wealth and power. People who've already indicated a willingness to kill and manipulate to get their way. Not the kind of people you want to bestow with that much power and influence." Jesse closed the article he'd been reading and went back to the search engine. "You know what keeps nagging at me?"

"What?"

"Those guys who were following us this afternoon had SSU written all over them. And if we're right that it was Katrina Hilliard's name that man in the street was saying, how does he know her?"

"Maybe she hired him."

"Maybe. But how would she know how to contact them? I mean, we've been trying to pull together all the threads connecting individual operatives with the parent company, AfterAssets, and we've been hitting brick wall after brick wall. So how would Katrina Hilliard know how to find those guys?"

"Maybe they approached her," Evie suggested.

"But why? How would they have known she was in the market for their services? We can't even connect her definitively to the Espera Group so far. There has to be some other connection. Something that would give her extra access to the services the SSU has been selling to the highest bidder."

"Well, what do we know about her background?" Evie waved at the computer. "Can you find an online bio?"

He typed *Katrina Hilliard bio* into the search box. A list of hits popped onto the screen, including the official White House bio. He clicked that one and found a dry, formal biographical sketch of the chief of staff, including a recent photograph.

Katrina Hilliard was an attractive African-American woman in her early forties. Slim and stunning in a deep red power suit in her official photo, she oozed confidence and competence. He scanned her credentials, stopping for a second on one particular line. "Did you realize she was at the Department of Energy before Cambridge tapped her as his chief of staff?"

Evie tugged her chair closer, her clean, warm scent making his head swim for a second. In that moment, he wished they were somewhere safe and secluded, with beautiful mountain views and a big, soft bed to share. Anywhere but here, holed up in a borrowed apartment with danger all around and a million reasons not to give in to the attraction zinging between them.

So, so many reasons.

"Interesting," Evie said. "Makes me wonder—"

"If she's the woman Morris Gamble's having an affair with?" Jesse finished for her. "Yeah, that crossed my mind, too. I'll put in a call to that number Nicholas Darcy gave us. Maybe he can run down some more information about their connection—"

"Whoa," Evie interrupted, staring at the computer screen.

"What?" He tried to follow her gaze, but the lines of credentials seemed to run together in front of his tired eyes.

She pointed at a line near the bottom of the screen. "'Hilliard spent three years on the board of the Singer Foundation,'" she read aloud. "Doesn't that ring any bells for you?"

"It's a security-affairs think tank," he said. "A few of my Marine buddies have done some work for them over the years."

"Several of my father's former colleagues did consulting work for them as well after their retirements, which is how I know that Jackson Melville was also on the Singer Foundation board around the time Hilliard was. There was a huge stink about it when MacLear went down and Melville was indicted for his crimes."

"So Hilliard would have known Melville pretty well."

She nodded. "I can't say for sure they were close, but they'd have known each other."

Jesse rubbed his jaw, his mind speeding through the implications. "And if she needed, for some reason, to get her hands on some amoral guns for hire, she'd know just who to ask."

"We need to find out if she ever visited Melville in prison," Evie suggested. The former MacLear CEO remained in custody pending his trial because the judge had deemed him a flight risk.

"I'm not sure how we do that without official imprimatur."

"Then let's get it."

"Small problem—we're sort of on the run."

She looked up at him, frustration shining in her blue eyes. "Right."

He caught her hand, giving it a squeeze. "We don't have to solve this mystery tonight. It's been a long, hellish day, and I don't know about you, but my eyes are starting to cross. Why don't we just call it a night and try to get some sleep?"

Her expression fell briefly, before she hid her emotions behind a carefully neutral mask. "Okay."

"Unless you don't want to get some sleep?"

She slanted a look at him. "No, I'm beat."

"I know. But maybe you're a little scared to close your eyes?"

She breathed a long, deep sigh. "You don't have to baby me. I'm fine."

"Considering what you witnessed this afternoon, there's no way you can be fine. I've been in battle, Evie. I've seen plenty of people die in terrible ways, and even I'm still dealing with what we saw today. It's okay to need time to process it all."

"What am I supposed to do, stay awake all night to avoid more bad dreams?" She shook her head. "We have so much we still don't know about what's going on and so little time to find out. I have to get some sleep or I'll be useless."

"Maybe I could find something here to help you sleep—"

"No, I don't want to be drugged. What if someone came after us here?"

He pushed a chunk of coppery hair out of her eyes. "I'd protect you."

"Who'd protect *you?*" Frustration creased her brow. "We don't know if there's really anyone we can trust here, including our friend with the DSS—"

He brushed his fingertips against her lips, silencing her midsentence. "I'm trained to defend myself and others."

Her lips trembled beneath his fingers, and the fire blazing in the depths of her blue eyes had nothing to do with fear. Jesse felt an answering lick of flame, low in his gut. A stream of images flooded his imagination—Evie's soft, curvy body, naked and hot, twined with his until he couldn't tell where he stopped and she began. Her hands, small and talented, moving with skill and imagination over his body. Her soft mouth, open and wet beneath his, her tongue dancing sinuously against his.

Wanting Evie was still...strange. Not because she wasn't beautiful or desirable—any man with eyes in his head and a working libido could have figured that out at first glance. But he'd seen her as Rita's little sister for so long that he had thought himself immune to her charms.

Clearly, as the kiss last night and the even more sexually intense kiss this afternoon had proved, he wasn't immune at all.

Evie stepped away from him suddenly, breaking the contact between them. "I guess I should at least try to get some sleep." Her gaze locked with his for a brief, electric moment, then she headed for the bedroom.

He watched her leave, his chest aching. The urge to stop her, to catch her and pull her back to him, stunned him with its intensity.

Just how out of control was he becoming where Evie was concerned?

EVIE WAS DROWNING. She couldn't see the water in the blackness surrounding her, but she could feel it, pouring into her mouth and ears, filling her lungs, smothering her. She struggled against the relentless tide, looking for an escape, a point of light, something to tell her there was hope in the middle of this terrifying black void.

A hand caught her arm, and she whipped around, torn between fear of the unknown and relief that she was no longer alone. The relief fled, the fear magnified as she found herself staring at Alan Wilson, the security guard her father had assigned to take her to her sister's wedding reception. He stared back at her, blood streaming from the bullet hole in his forehead.

She tried to pull away from his tight grip, but something behind her blocked her retreat. She twisted frantically, finally pulling free from Wilson's grasp, only to find herself tangled up in the shattered limbs of the SSU agent who'd tried to chase her across Martin Luther King Boulevard.

"Jesse!" she tried to scream, but only gurgles emerged from her throat. Her head swam, her heart pounding so hard and fast that she feared it would burst out of her chest.

"I'm here." Jesse's voice seemed to come from miles away, barely audible. She turned around and around, desperate to find where the voice was coming from.

"Jesse?" Her throat was no longer filled with water but with sand. It rasped over her vocal cords as she tried to speak, filled her mouth with the dry heat of the desert.

"Right here, Evie. Open your eyes." Jesse's voice was louder now, close by. He'd told her to open her eyes, but she hadn't realized they were closed. Blinking them open, she expected to see a bright, relentless desert sun, burning down on her with its desiccated heat.

Instead, she opened her eyes to cool darkness relieved by pale streaks of blue moonlight filtering through a nearby window. She was on a pillowy mattress, swaddled in soft sheets and a fluffy comforter.

And Jesse was there, in the dark, a comforting shadow sitting on the edge of her bed.

"I'm sorry," she murmured, her voice raspy with sleep. Her mouth was dry, her throat aching for something to drink. "I woke you."

He touched her hand, his fingers warm on her skin. "I wasn't asleep yet. It's only eleven. You were having a bad dream."

She tried to remember what she'd been dreaming about. She could recall only a few strange snippets—the sensation of drowning, the escalating terror of feeling trapped and unable to move away from the danger. A flash of blood on a man's face, of twisted limbs and bleeding grins—

She drove those images away, squelching a shudder. "I don't remember what it was about."

"Well, why don't you try to get back to sleep, then? Maybe this time you'll have sweet dreams."

"I need to get something to drink first."

"Stay here. I'll get it for you." He was up off the bed and out the door before she could protest. With a sigh, she pulled herself into a sitting position and turned on the lamp on the bedside table, driving the darkness to the corners of the room.

Jesse came back with a glass of ice water and a small plastic pitcher. He set them both on the bedside table. "If you get thirsty in the night, you won't have to get up and wake yourself up."

She smiled, touched by his thoughtfulness. He was really making it hard to put her schoolgirl fantasies about him behind her. "Thank you."

"No problem."

As he started to get up, she caught his hand. "Shouldn't you be in bed? We could both use some sleep."

He looked down at her, his eyes coffee-dark. "I was doing a little more research into Katrina Hilliard's background."

"Oh?" She let go of his hand and patted the edge of the bed next to her.

He accepted her invitation to sit. "I decided to do a search for her name and Jackson Melville's together. And it turns out the Singer Foundation Board wasn't their only connection. They both were at Princeton the same years, and I found an interview with Hilliard from ten years ago, before MacLear's fall, where Hilliard was praising Melville for MacLear's expansion into environmental recovery as part of the services they offered."

She arched an eyebrow. "MacLear offered environmental-recovery services?"

"It was news to me, too. I called Rick to ask him about it. Apparently they offered manpower for things like oil-spill cleanups and other environmental disasters. But Rick thinks it might have been a cover for getting the SSU into some sensitive areas."

"I would have figured Hilliard as someone deeply suspicious of mercenary outfits like MacLear. Based on her other known viewpoints."

"A lot of ideological people look the other way when it comes to supporting their own pet projects."

"You mean she would have turned a blind eye to what the SSU was doing as long as their actions supported her goals?"

"You don't get to a position like chief of staff to the president without making a few compromises along the way," Jesse said.

"Murder is a pretty big compromise."

"The ends justify the means for some people."

Evie shivered. "I can't imagine thinking like that."

"I know you can't. I saw how you reacted to what happened to those men today." Jesse brushed a piece of her hair away from her eyes.

Heat flooded the narrow space between them, and Evie's body responded with a flush of intense sexual awareness. His fingers brushing against the skin of her forehead felt like a caress. His dark eyes locked with hers, desire burning in their depths.

He wanted her. She wanted him. What to do next seemed so simple and effortless.

Only it wasn't. It might be effortless, but it could never be simple. Not when she was Rita's sister and he was the man who'd broken her sister's heart, even if, ultimately, the breakup had been no one's fault.

He cleared his throat and stood up, snapping the exquisite tension between them. She leaned back against the headboard, feeling boneless.

"I made that call to Darcy, but he was a step ahead of us. He'd already been looking into the story about Morris Gamble's affair and came up with Katrina Hilliard as the top prospect for the role of the other woman."

"Really? How?"

"That's the interesting part. He said his sources mentioned seeing Gamble meeting Hilliard around lunchtime outside a house in Congress Heights every Wednesday, Thursday and Friday for weeks. He checked the address—it belongs to Hilliard's aunt, the one who works at St. Elizabeth's."

"Every Wednesday through Friday?"

He nodded.

"So what do we do next? Go stake out that neighborhood and try to catch them in the act?" She couldn't help but sound doubtful. They'd already

dodged bullets doing something a lot less dangerous than that.

"Actually, I don't think there's much else to find
here in D.C.," he said.

His statement caught her by surprise. "I thought
you said the answers to our questions were here."

"And they were. But they didn't really solve our
bigger problem, did they? The SSU is still coming
after you."

"Then what good did it do to come here?" She felt
queasy at the thought that all they'd gone through
over the past few days had been without a purpose.
Two men had died because they'd come here. They
might have been very bad guys, but had they de-
served to die such horrible, bloody deaths? "Did
we do it all for nothing?"

He leaned against the doorframe, his gaze
thoughtful. "It wasn't for nothing. We have a pretty
good idea that at least two of the president's most
trusted advisers have thrown in with the Espera
Group's goals. And it's good that we know about
Katrina Hilliard's links to Jackson Melville, even
if we can't prove she's behind what the SSU has
been doing."

"If we can't prove it, we can't stop her."

"We're not through trying to prove it." His voice
was resolute. "It's just time we take a different
tack."

"Like what?"

"There's a reason the bad guys have been going

to such lengths to find General Ross's journal. Clearly they believe the journal contains the kind of evidence we're looking for."

Evie's gut tightened as a terrible thought occurred to her. "Do you think that's why Mrs. Ross was attacked? They were looking for the journal at her house?"

Jesse's mouth tightened with anger. "Shannon said they tore up her house pretty badly. They were looking for *something*. It could have been the journal, I suppose."

"But you haven't exactly been shy about letting people know the journal's in Cooper Security's possession," she pointed out. "Why would they be looking for it at Mrs. Ross's house?"

"Maybe they're looking for the code instead. Finding the journal doesn't help at all if you don't have all three portions of the code. They've been trying to go after you as a way to force your father to reveal his part of the code, and they kidnapped the whole Harlowe family for three weeks in hope of getting the general to give them his code key. They're going after everything as ruthlessly as they can."

And they could be very ruthless, Evie thought, remembering Alan Wilson's blood staining the upholstery of his SUV. She couldn't hold back a little shudder. "So what do we do now, if we've accomplished all we can here in D.C.?"

He pushed away from the doorframe, squaring

his shoulders and meeting her questioning gaze with firm resolve.

"It's time to go home," he said.

Chapter Thirteen

Jesse and Evie drove across the state line between Virginia and Tennessee a little before five Thursday afternoon, after a late start that morning leaving Annie Harlowe's apartment in Arlington. Evie had wanted to make sure they gave the place a good cleaning before they left.

"I can arrange for someone to come clean after we leave," Jesse had told her, amused by her nervous energy as she washed dishes, wiped down counters and scrubbed the tub.

"I want to do it myself. I know Annie personally, and if she ever gets a chance to get out of that safe house and back here to D.C., I want to be able to say I left her place in better condition than I found it."

He'd caught her hands as she started to pull out a mop for the kitchen floor. "Evie, you're just delaying the inevitable. We have to go back home today. It's where the journal is."

She'd put the mop back in the closet and pressed her cheek against his shoulder, melting into his embrace when he'd put his arms around her and pulled her close. "Have you heard anything new on Mrs. Ross's condition?"

"I talked to Shannon early this morning before you woke up," he'd told her, trying to keep his caress comforting instead of seductive. "No change so far, but the doctors tell her that it's actually a good sign that her condition hasn't deteriorated. Her chances of recovery improve every hour she doesn't get any worse."

He'd checked with Shannon again when they'd stopped outside Roanoke for lunch, and learned, to his relief, that Lydia Ross was starting to wake up. "The doctors can't promise she won't have some memory issues," Shannon had cautioned, but she hadn't been able to keep the excitement out of her voice. During the week she'd spent on Nightshade Island with Lydia Ross and her right-hand man, Gideon Stone, Shannon had become fast friends with the general's widow. And she'd fallen head over heels in love with Stone, a former Marine who had made protecting Lydia Ross, whose son had died saving Gideon's life, his personal mission.

Shannon and Lydia had stayed in touch after Lydia left the island and moved to Burkettville, a small farming town just north of Gossamer Ridge. She and Shannon visited back and forth often, because the drive between the two towns took only ten minutes.

The attack on Lydia had hit Shannon and Gideon

hard, Jesse knew, well beyond her connection to the mystery Cooper Security was trying to solve. He was rather fond of the woman himself, admiring her combination of guts and grace. If he'd stayed in the Marine Corps, he'd have been smart to find such a woman as his wife.

His gaze wandered over to Evie, who was driving this leg of the trip. In a lot of ways, she reminded him of Lydia Ross, far more than Rita ever had. Rita was smart and resourceful, brilliantly beautiful and utterly charming. But she lacked her younger sister's dogged determination, her scrappy confidence and her strength in the face of fear.

Evie's charms were buried a little deeper than her sister's. But now that he had begun to understand just what kind of woman she really was, behind the occasional prickly self-protection, he found himself thinking that she was the superior sister.

Unnerved by that realization, he dragged his thoughts back to more immediate concerns. "Pull off at the next exit," he said.

She glanced his way. "What are we going to do?"

"Load our guns. We're in reciprocity territory now." Unlike Virginia, Tennessee would honor their concealed carry permits. And he'd already spent too long feeling naked and unprotected. He wasn't the sort of man who shot first and asked questions later, but he had run into enough trouble over the years to know that he was safer armed than not.

They had to drive a long way before they came

to the next exit, then another few miles before Jesse spotted a narrow country lane that looked secluded enough for their purposes. "Pull off there," he said, pointing.

They dug their weapons from the trunk of the car and loaded them with fresh ammunition. Jesse chambered an extra round, and Evie followed suit. She lifted the hem of her shirt, giving him an all-too-brief look at her flat stomach as she slid her hip holster into place and tucked the compact Ruger she carried into the holder.

He dragged his gaze away and holstered his GLOCK, dropping the hem of his denim jacket over the bulge of his weapon. Overhead, the sky was leaden, moisture adding a bite to the mild October air. "I should have checked the weather reports before we left D.C."

Evie looked up at the gunmetal-gray clouds above them. "I did. Supposed to be heavy rain this afternoon all across the area." She dropped her gaze to meet his. "We're still four and a half hours away from Maybridge. Are you sure we should try to get there tonight?"

Temptation licked at his belly. "We could find a motel somewhere around here."

"Another no-tell motel?" she asked with a half grimace.

"I'd rather not sleep in a place you have to fumigate first," he admitted. "But those are the kinds of places that will take cash, nobody asks too many questions and they keep their mouths shut when the law comes knocking."

She released a soft breath. "You're right."

Thunder rumbled from the south. "Sounds like we'll be heading straight into it."

"Then we'd better get a move on." Evie tossed him the keys. "You drive."

He caught the keys and circled around to the driver's side.

"Are you glad to be going home?" Evie asked a few miles later.

He glanced at her. She was gazing forward through the windshield, presenting him with her pretty profile. "I'll be glad to have my family around," he admitted.

"Safety in numbers?"

"Something like that."

"Did we do the right thing? Going to D.C.?"

He wondered if she was still thinking about the two men who'd died in the street in Congress Heights. That morning, before leaving D.C., they'd bought a newspaper and learned that both men had succumbed to their injuries. "You don't still blame yourself for what happened to those two men, do you?"

"No, but they'd still be alive if we'd never gone there."

"They'd still be alive if they hadn't chased us into traffic with guns," Jesse told her flatly. "They chose their own path."

She fell silent for the next few miles, stirring only when Jesse pulled off the interstate in Knoxville, heading southeast toward the airport. "Where are we going?"

"Best cheap motels are almost always near an airport," he said.

"'Best cheap motels' being a relative term," she murmured, stretching her arms and legs. The movement stretched her T-shirt tight across her small, firm breasts, reminding him that the luxury of staying in a place with two bedrooms was about to be over.

They found a small, slightly shabby motel just north of the airport. The Volunteer Inn offered little in the way of amenities—no pool, no internet, only the most basic of cable. But Jesse's Bluetooth worked fine in their small, two-bed room, giving them internet access at least.

He set up the laptop while Evie examined the bedding with a critical eye. "You know bedbugs are on the rise, right?" she asked as she pulled one of the thin blankets away from the sheets beneath.

"Yeah, ask me about the camel spiders in Iraq," he answered.

She slanted a look his way. "You never talk about Iraq. Or Afghanistan or Kaziristan—"

"Or the Sudan or Sanselmo or Colombia," he added, keeping his voice light. "So?"

"Why not?"

"What is there to talk about? War is hell."

"Rita said you kept things bottled up. All the time. She'd try to get you to share your feelings and experiences with her but you'd just clam up."

He turned from the laptop to look at her. "Rita didn't want to hear my experiences."

"But—"

"No buts. I tried to tell her sometimes. But I could see what it did to her, hearing the kind of hell we all had to face in the battle zone. It hurt her. Scared her. Your father knew the same thing about her. He kept that part of his life away from your family, didn't he?"

She dropped the blanket back in place and sat on the edge of the bed nearest to him, her hands folded almost primly on her lap. "Yes, he did. Remember how I told you I wanted to be a Marine? Well, after I announced my plans to him and Mom, he sat me down and shared a little about what he'd gone through in the first Gulf War and in Panama. It was pretty terrifying, hearing how close he came to dying so many times."

"It's why we don't talk about it," he said quietly.

"But I can take it."

He leaned toward her, covering her hands with one of his own. "I know. You're one of the strongest people I know."

She turned one hand over, curling her fingers over his. "I'm not sure that's true. Sometimes I feel as if I'm drowning and I can't find the surface."

He squeezed her hand. "Sometimes I feel the same way."

She laughed softly. "No, you don't. You always know what you want and how to get it. And then you go do it. No fuss, no muss."

He laughed, as well. "Apparently I hide my neuroses well."

One dark eyebrow lifted, and her blue eyes sparkled with curiosity. "What neuroses might those be?"

"Well," he admitted, "I'm not fond of spiders."

"Like camel spiders?"

"Exactly. And I'm obsessive about winning."

She grinned. "I know. I've played poker with you. Really, taking a week's allowance from a seventeen-year-old? Harsh, Cooper. Very harsh."

"You knew what you were getting into. And if you'd won, you'd have gotten me as your personal slave for a month."

"Oh, that would have been nice," she said with a wistful smile.

"Yeah? What would you have ordered me to do?"

She pretended to give it some thought. "Change Tuffy's litter box, for one thing."

He grimaced. "What else?"

"Well, the reason I really made the bet was that my senior prom was coming up, and I didn't have a date." She shot him a sheepish half smile.

Her answer surprised him. "You'd have made me take you to your senior prom?"

Her smile faded. "You don't have to make it sound like a fate worse than Tuffy's litter box."

"I'm sorry," he said quickly. "I didn't mean it that way. I just—why? There had to be a dozen teenage guys beating down your door back then. Why would you want to take your sister's boyfriend?"

She looked down at their entwined hands. "Because I saw you first."

He waited for her to continue. She looked up at him, finally, her cheeks flushed and her eyes dark with humiliation.

"I met you first, remember? I was with my father on his first tour of the new base, and you were assigned to give him a quick tour before he met with the rest of the base command at the officer's mess."

"I remember." She'd been all arms, legs and thick, dark braids. Her curves hadn't developed at that age, and her shy smile had reminded him of his youngest sister, Shannon, who was only a year younger than Evie. "You were quiet."

"I was smitten," she said quietly. "I could barely breathe around you."

"I didn't know."

"I know you didn't. I worked hard to make sure you never did."

"You were so young then."

"Just three years younger than Rita."

"But there's a big difference between seventeen and twenty. And I was twenty-six. Some of my fellow Marines accused me of cradle robbing when I asked Rita out the first time."

She pulled her hand away from him. "I know."

"How long did the crush last?" It wasn't the question he'd intended to ask, but he found himself curious to hear her answer.

She lifted her gaze slowly to meet his. Her blue eyes smoldered, igniting a wildfire in his own veins. "I don't think it's ever ended."

He pulled his chair closer, taking both of her hands in his own. "Are you sure about that?"

"You've kissed me twice and you have to ask?"

He smiled a little at her tone of voice. "Desire is physical. What you're talking about is emotional."

"For me, they go hand in hand."

He wasn't surprised by her words. Evie Marsh had always struck him as the kind of woman who took things like sex and love seriously. She wouldn't be able to separate those two things as lightly as some people did.

He'd never been very good at separating sex and love either. Oh, he'd indulged his physical desires quite a few times over the years without feeling much of an emotional connection to his partner. But bad sex with someone he loved was better than the best sex he had with someone he didn't really care about.

"It would be easier if they didn't," he said quietly, feeling as if he owed her the bare truth.

"Why?"

He brushed his knuckles over her cheek, feeling a surge of raw masculine pleasure as she leaned into his touch like a purring cat. "Because we could get naked and go at it right now without any fear or regret. And I've got to tell you, Evie Marsh, I'd really like to get you naked right now."

Her eyes darkened. "What's stopping you?"

He couldn't come up with a good answer. His mind was too busy taking off her clothes and exploring every silken curve of her body. He wanted to kiss his way across her body, down the satiny curve of her thighs and along the well-toned length of her slender arms. He could almost feel her beneath him, hot and slick and welcoming, her legs wrapping around his back to pull him deeper inside her.

She put her hand in the center of his chest, flattening her palm over his heart. "I don't need to be protected from you. I'm not seventeen anymore."

He covered her hand with his, trapping it against his racing heart. "Feel what you do to me?"

She nodded slowly. "Yes."

He lowered his head, brushing his mouth against hers. Her lips parted, inviting him to deepen the kiss. Their tongues clashed, then found a seductive rhythm of give-and-take, reminding him how much he wanted—needed—to be inside her.

He told himself to go slow, to give her pleasure first before seeking his own, but Evie's small, talented hands were driving him beyond reason, moving over his hips to tease his buttocks until he was harder than he could ever remember being.

"Evie," he growled as she slid her hand between their bodies to cup him firmly through his jeans.

"Shh," she breathed against the side of his neck, nipping the tendon until he bucked helplessly against her hand.

He wasn't a teenager, damn it. He was good at seduction. He wasn't supposed to be the one trembling and weak, but here he was, shaking like a virgin, both terrified and enthralled by her power over him.

He slid his thumb over her tight nipple, caressing through the thin layers of cotton T-shirt and silk bra. She moaned against his collarbone, and he felt his own power surge to life.

He unzipped her jeans in one movement, slipping his hand beneath the denim and silk barrier between his fingers and her soft sex. She gasped as he touched her, clutching his arms as she arched her back in response. A low, guttural profanity escaped her lips, making him laugh.

He withdrew his hand, earning another hissing curse, and grabbed the hem of her T-shirt, drawing it up over her head. She reached for the front hook of her bra but he stopped her, closing his hand over hers.

"Leave it," he whispered, bending his head to kiss the curve of her breast just above the silk of her bra. "For now."

She curled her fingers through his hair, drawing his mouth lower. He slid his tongue over her pebbled nipple, laved it through the silk until she was panting softly, her back arching in a half circle.

He kissed his way to the other breast, gently tugging the nipple with his teeth. Then he moved lower, over the shadowy contours of her rib cage, down the narrow furrow of muscle until his tongue ran lightly over the rim of her belly button.

She let go of his hair and clutched handfuls of the bedspread in her white-knuckled fists. Her hips writhed against him. "Jesse—please—"

The trill of a cell phone filtered through the haze after a couple of rings. His body screamed at him to ignore it, but his inner Marine ordered him to do his duty. He'd made protecting Evie Marsh his mission. He meant to see it through, at any cost.

He drew away from her, sitting up on the side of the bed.

"No!" Evie moaned. "Let it ring."

"I can't." He willed his body under control and grabbed the phone from his duffel bag. "Yeah?"

It was his sister Shannon. "Lydia's awake."

Evie sat up beside him, gathering her T-shirt in front of her in an endearing display of belated modesty. He wanted to kiss away the frustrated furrow creasing her brow. "How is she?" he asked his sister.

"Better than we hoped. She remembers what happened."

He looked at Evie. "Lydia remembers what happened," he told her. Into the phone, he asked, "Did she recognize her attackers?"

"No, but she remembered they were after her jewelry."

Her answer surprised him. "Just petty thieves, then?"

"No," Shannon answered. "They told her they knew her husband had put the code in her locket. They demanded she give it to them."

"Her locket?"

"She has a locket the general gave her not long before he died. She wears it all the time."

His heart dropped. "Did they get it?"

"That's the lucky break." Shannon sounded pleased. "A couple of days before the home invasion, Lydia broke the clasp and took it to a jeweler to be fixed. It's safe and sound—Gideon and I got it from the jeweler an hour ago and took it to the vault at the office for safekeeping."

"What about the code?"

"We think it's in a hidden compartment beneath the photo. We thought you should be here when we try to open it. How soon can you be here?"

He looked at his watch. "We can be there by midnight."

Evie looked up at him as he hung up the phone, clutching her T-shirt more tightly against her chest. She looked soft and seductive without even trying, and his body tightened with hunger. "What's going on?" she asked.

He made himself move away from her, crossing to the window table to unplug his laptop. "We think we've found General Ross's part of the code." He turned to look at her, hoping she saw the regret and lingering desire in his eyes. "We have to go home tonight."

Chapter Fourteen

The four-hour drive to Chickasaw County turned into almost five hours, as the threatened autumn thunderstorms unleashed their fury on them all the way into Alabama. Evie had been happy to let Jesse drive in the rain, but she hadn't reckoned on Jesse's lingering silence. Visibility was wretched, giving him a very good reason to concentrate on the road ahead without speaking, but no radio and no conversation made for an interminable ride and gave Evie plenty of time to worry about the consequences of letting Jesse Cooper seduce her.

Was he regretting it now? She found his still, focused expression impossible to read. He gave every appearance of concentrating on nothing but the road ahead, but she knew from experience that he had one hell of a poker face. His mysterious eyes and the tempting allure of secret intentions lurking beneath his expressionless face had always been one of the most attractive things about him.

She could try to engage him, but dread kept her

silent. Jesse had told her already how impossible it would be for the two of them to have any kind of romantic relationship.

You're Rita's sister.

The inevitable roadblock, she thought with a hint of bitterness, not at her sister or even at Jesse but at her own dogged determination to ignore all the warning signs that should have sent her running away from Jesse Cooper years ago.

Jesse was the one who finally broke the silence as they crossed the Chickasaw County line. "Home, sweet home."

"Where do we go next?" she asked quietly.

He looked at her for the first time in hours. "Shannon said she and Gideon would meet us at Cooper Security so we could take a crack at the locket right away."

She looked at her watch. It was nearing midnight, but she was too wound up to sleep anyway. "What about security at the office?"

She'd been working late at Cooper Security just last month when a group of SSU commandos had stormed the place, looking for both the coded journal and Annie Harlowe. Annie had escaped their captivity a few days earlier and was helping Cooper Security try to find her missing parents.

Evie, Annie and Jesse's brother Wade had barely escaped the building through the roof exit before the gun-wielding intruders had burst onto the roof behind him. Fortunately for the three of them, Jesse had already gone for help, bringing his cousin J.D., a former Navy chopper pilot, and Cooper Security's shiny Bell 407 helicopter to the rescue.

"I've called in extra security," he told her. "I also asked Rick to ask your father to come. I'd like him to be there tonight if we find the other part of the code."

She frowned. "I'm not sure he'll come."

"Maybe if he realizes we already have the other two codes, he'll see it's safer to share what he knows than to stay silent."

"What if the code isn't in the locket?"

"It's got to be."

"But what if it's not?" He'd explained to her what Shannon had told him about Lydia Ross's locket. "How did the SSU even know to look for the locket? Even Lydia Ross had no idea the code might be in the locket."

"I don't know," Jesse admitted. "Maybe they've been doing the same thing we've been doing, trying to figure out who he'd have trusted with the code. I've always wondered why General Ross didn't tell Gideon about the code, because he trusted him enough to share his suspicions about what happened to Ford."

Just over two years ago, the Rosses' son, Ford, had died in a grenade attack in Kaziristan, where he and Gideon Stone had been part of a Marine Corps unit supporting NATO peacekeepers. But this was the first Evie had heard of the general's suspicions. "What kind of suspicions?" she asked.

"Oh, I forgot you wouldn't know." He shot her a look of apology. "General Ross believed the SSU, rather than al Adar rebels, launched the grenade that killed Ford."

"My God." She lifted her hand to her suddenly aching throat. "Why would they do that?"

"I think they already knew the generals were looking into what they were up to in Kaziristan. They'd already broken a hell of a lot of laws, international and otherwise, to put the Espera Group's preferred leaders into power. The general thought they killed Ford as a warning to him."

"To keep him from looking any further into their activities?"

"Exactly."

"I wonder if they threatened Lydia's life, too. Might explain why the general never entrusted her with the code. He'd have wanted to protect her."

"I'm sure he kept her out of the loop precisely to protect her," Jesse said firmly. "He loved her. He wouldn't have wanted to put her neck on the line. Not even to stop the Espera Group conspiracy."

They turned down the long, wooded road to the Cooper Security office complex, a sprawling four-story building nestled in the middle of dense woodlands on the edge of Maybridge, the Chickasaw County seat. Evie's apartment was only a mile away in the small town's center, but most of the Coopers still lived in and around Gossamer Ridge, the lake-side town where they'd grown up.

When Cooper Security came into view, the whole complex was lit up like a Christmas tree, dozens of vehicles lining the parking lot. "You're going to have a lot of overtime to pay this month," Evie murmured.

"Most of these folks are salaried," he replied with a slight smile. He headed for his reserved parking spot near the side entrance. Before he'd even cut the engine, four suit-clad Cooper Security guards flanked the car, their watchful eyes scanning the parking lot and the woods beyond for trouble.

The show of force should have made Evie feel more secure, but it only served to raise her anxiety level. If Jesse had ordered this kind of security, they must be in grave danger indeed.

Jesse's sister Shannon and Gideon Stone met them at the door. Shannon threw her arms around her brother, her brown eyes shining with relief. "Rick told us about what happened yesterday in D.C. It must have been a nightmare."

Gideon shook Jesse's hand. "Glad to have you back, boss."

Shannon turned to Evie. "We thought you might want to shower and change after the long drive. We've put some things for the two of you in a couple of the dorm rooms. On the second floor," she added to her brother, handing him a couple of keys.

"Rooms 218 and 220. Rick's waiting for you in 218 for a debriefing."

"Any luck getting my father here?" Evie asked, not expecting an affirmative answer.

"Actually, he's already here. So's your mom. They're with their security detail up in the conference room," Shannon answered.

"Come on, let's get cleaned up and changed." Jesse guided her toward the glassed-in bridge connecting the main office building with the dormitory, a four-story block of sleeping rooms designed to offer Cooper Security personnel and their families shelter in case of a natural disaster or terrorist attack. Agents also used the rooms when they were working long shifts, saving time and fuel by bunking down on the Cooper Security grounds.

Jesse unlocked the door to Evie's assigned room and took a quick look around inside before he turned back to Evie. "I'll be right next door."

She almost caught his hand and asked him not to go, resisting only by clenching her fists so hard that her fingernails dented the flesh of her palms. "Don't head back over there without me."

His smile faded, and the look he gave her was intense and deadly serious. "I won't." He caught one of her hands, gently opened her clenched fist and put her room key on her palm.

Then he was gone, the door closing with a soft click behind him.

Evie took a quick shower and dressed in the fresh

jeans and clean gray blouse Shannon had laid out for her on the dormitory bed. Leaving her thrift-store weekender bag and its stash of secondhand clothes on the bed, she ventured into the hallway to see if Jesse was done with his own cleanup.

She found him in the corridor outside her room, his head bent in quiet conversation with his brother Rick. At the sound of her door opening, he turned to look at her, his expression troubled.

"What's going on?" she asked, her stomach knotting.

"We haven't heard from the agents we sent to Spain to keep an eye on your sister and her new husband since yesterday morning, so we've sent out an alert to some of our contacts in Europe. We're waiting for word."

"What about Rita and Andrew?"

"We can't confirm their whereabouts either."

Evie covered her mouth. "Oh, God."

"Your parents just tried calling the number she gave them when they arrived in Barcelona. It's seven-thirty in the morning in Spain, but they're not answering." Jesse looked grim.

She tried to look for a more positive spin. "They're newlyweds. Maybe they're otherwise occupied."

"Maybe," Jesse agreed, his gaze smoldering as he lifted his eyes to lock with hers. An answering heat licked at her belly, notching her heart rate higher as the image of his strong, talented hands moving over her flesh drove out, momentarily, even her growing alarm about her sister's safety.

Rick interrupted her thoughts with a much-needed reality check. "We need to get to the war room and see what we can sort out."

He led the way, Jesse sticking close to Evie. Her skin prickled as they hurried down the long connecting corridor between the dorms and the offices. She knew the glass itself was bullet resistant, and that Jesse and his family had tightened perimeter security after the SSU invasion last month, but she couldn't help walking more quickly than normal, feeling exposed. It was a relief to reach the safety of the other side, where interior walls provided extra protection from sniper fire.

In the conference room, several people had already gathered, including Evie's parents. Her father spotted her first, his eyes widening with delight. He hurried over to her, wrapping her in a tight hug.

"Evie Marsh, I ought to strangle you for scaring your mother and me like this!" He caught her cheeks between his big hands and kissed her forehead. "Are you all right?"

"I'm fine," she assured him.

He tugged her short red hair. "What the hell did you do to your hair?"

"Your fault for practically putting my face on a milk carton."

Her father's gaze slanted toward Jesse, and the relief that had lightened his blue eyes faded into anger. "Cooper, what the hell were you thinking, taking her with you?"

"I made him take me," Evie said quickly. She could see the news about Rita had put Jesse in no mood to argue with her father. "And it's a good thing, too. I happen to think I was a big help."

"She was," Jesse agreed.

"I thought it was clear I didn't want you to take her off with you. That's why I did the whole song and dance about her being kidnapped. You should have stopped her from going with you."

Jesse exchanged a glance with Evie. "I've learned that your daughter prefers to make her own decisions for herself."

"Hogwash." Her father shook his head. "First you break Rita's heart, now you put Evie in danger—"

"Bax, stop." Evie's mother, Donna, put her hand on her husband's arm. "Let's concentrate on finding Rita and worry about everything else later." She pulled Evie into a tight embrace. "I think your hair looks adorable. But don't you ever scare us this way again!"

"Anything new?" Rick Cooper asked his sister Isabel, who had been waiting with the Marshes in the conference room.

Her husband, Ben Scanlon, stood near one of the windows, gazing out on the rainy night. He turned at Rick's question and answered for Isabel. "We haven't heard anything from Rita and Andrew. And Delilah and Terry still haven't checked in."

"What does that mean?" Evie's father asked.

"It doesn't have to be bad news," Evie answered before any of the others could. "It's protocol if there's a suspected threat for our operatives to get the clients to a place of safety. This may include going incommunicado if they believe communications could compromise their safety."

"That could very well be what's happened," Jesse agreed, quirking his eyebrows at Evie.

What, she thought, *you thought I didn't listen during the training courses?*

"Why don't we get caught up to date on what Shannon and Gideon have found?" Jesse watched his youngest sister walk through the door carrying a small box. "Is that the locket?"

Shannon opened the box and set it on the conference room table. "We think there's a secret compartment behind the photo, but it seems to have been soldered shut. Gideon says he can open it, but we wanted you to take a look first."

Evie darted a quick look at Jesse, her lips curving. His brothers and sisters treated him more like a father than a brother sometimes. Evie supposed that was due to his having to take up so much of the slack in the family after his mother left. His father's deputy-sheriff position at the time had kept him constantly busy, leaving Jesse to play both mother and father to his younger siblings.

Jesse lifted the locket from the box and examined it closely. Evie edged closer to get a better look. The chain was nothing out of the ordinary, a series of simple gold links, but the locket itself was large, over two inches long by an inch and a half wide. The front of the locket was inlaid with painted enamel in the form of a peacock in full display.

"Beautiful," Evie murmured.

"Lydia loves it, so I'd rather we not destroy it trying to get to whatever's hidden inside," Shannon said.

"Reminds me of that locket Trey Prichard gave me," Jesse's sister Isabel said. "He was my best friend's brother," she explained to the Marshes. "After she died, he gave me the locket. Told me she'd wanted me to have it. It took years to figure out that the locket was a clue to who'd killed her."

"He'd put a key inside the locket," Isabel's husband, Ben, added. "It led to a storage locker where he'd stashed evidence that helped bring down a big meth and pot distribution racket."

"When was that?" Gideon asked curiously.

"Back in April."

He smiled slightly. "The general gave Lydia the locket in May. And I know he was very interested in the Swain family drug bust—he sent me all the way to Mobile to pick up every newspaper I could find that mentioned the bust. When I asked him why, he told me I'd understand sooner or later."

"The Swains had made connections with the SSU," Isabel said. "They were negotiating to help the SSU run guns through Bolen Bluff—they'd gotten as far as making contact with a Peruvian gun runner named Carlos Kurasawa."

Evie saw her father shift uncomfortably. "Dad, do you know anything about Carlos Kurasawa and the Swains?"

He looked at her, his lips pressed into a tight line.

"It doesn't matter," Jesse said, giving Evie a quick warning look. She tightened her own lips, annoyed that he was taking her father's side. They needed the information her father was sitting on, and Jesse was enabling him?

"Let me take a look at the locket," Evie's mother said.

Jesse handed it over.

Her mother pulled a pair of glasses from her bag and slipped them on, taking a close look at the locket. A smile curved her lips. "It's not soldered shut. It's a puzzle." She pressed the small pewter-colored bead four times and suddenly the gold backing popped open, revealing a small compartment inside.

"How did you—" Evie began, nearly speechless.

"When your father and I visited the Rosses on Nightshade Island this past spring, Lydia and Edward took us shopping. Baxter and Lydia went to the bookstore first, but I wanted to do some antiques shopping, and Edward was kind enough to accompany me. We found this very locket in a shop in Terrebonne, and the shop owner showed us how to get to the inner compartment." She handed the locket to Jesse. "I believe this may be what you're looking for.

Evie stepped closer to Jesse to see what lay inside the compartment.

"It's a memory card," Jesse said, carefully removing the small black card from the hidden compartment. As he started toward the laptop computer sitting on the end of the conference table, Shannon stopped him.

"Let me do it," she said. "In case there's some sort of trick to accessing the information on this card."

She slipped the card into the slot at the front of the laptop and waited to see if the computer could read whatever data the card held.

While everyone else gathered around the laptop, Evie noticed that her father had moved away from the crowd, gazing out at the rain-washed night. Torn between her curiosity about the memory card and compassion for her father, she finally dragged herself away from the others and joined her father at the window.

"I know you're worried about Rita—"

"I'm worried about all of you. Your sister, your mother and you."

"Is that why you won't tell us what you know?"

"What I know may be all that stands between Rita coming back to us alive or coming back to us in a body bag."

Evie shuddered. "We don't even know she's been taken."

He passed his hand over his face. Evie heard the scratch of his beard against his palm and realized he hadn't shaved that day. It was unlike her spit-and-polish father to let his personal grooming go that way.

"Is there no way to safely reach your people?" he asked.

"We've put out an alert, but we give them a forty-eight hour window to operate on their own before we send out actual searchers." Jesse's voice behind her made Evie jump.

She turned and found him watching her with curious eyes. "Any luck on the card?" she asked.

"Shannon says it has an encryption program written in that's keeping her from being able to open the file. She thinks she can work through the encryption, though it could take a while."

"You wait forty-eight hours before you go looking for your people when they go incommunicado?" Evie's father asked Jesse, looking appalled.

"This isn't the Marines, sir. In many ways, we behave more like covert ops. And in covert ops, you have to trust your people to know what they're doing. Rushing in and looking for them at this point could put them in greater danger if they're trying to lie low."

"It's also possible that Rita and her husband are simply not answering their phones for some reason," Isabel added, wandering up in time to hear her brother's reply. "Maybe they left the hotel for the day and forgot their phones back in the room."

"Or maybe Terry and I spotted a couple of guys on our SSU Most Wanted list and decided it was time to haul these two lovebirds back home."

All heads in the conference room swiveled toward the door, where Delilah Hammond leaned against the doorjamb, looking tired but pleased with herself. Behind her, Terry Allen rolled his eyes but grinned.

And next to them, looking tired but very much alive, were Rita and her husband, Andrew.

Chapter Fifteen

The two "lovebirds," as Delilah had called them, didn't look as happy. Rita's hair was a mess, she wasn't wearing a stitch of makeup, and her clothes looked slept in. Andrew, Evie noticed, was primarily concerned with Rita and her state of mind. So far, he was the kind of attentive, sensitive man her sister seemed to want in a husband. Evie hoped it would always remain so.

Everyone started talking at once. Evie's parents rushed forward to greet their other daughter, while Rick started asking a rapid-fire set of questions of the two Cooper Security agents.

Evie looked at Jesse and found him staring at Rita, relief in his eyes. She looked away, her chest aching.

As the din in the conference room grew into chaos, he stepped forward and took charge. "Okay, hold up. One at a time."

The room quieted down and Jesse turned to Delilah. "What happened?"

"We were watching the Joya del Mar Hotel early this morning when we spotted a couple of guys on the list of SSU operatives we've identified," Delilah answered in her distinctive Appalachian drawl. She was a tall, curvy woman in her thirties, with dusky shoulder-length hair currently tied up in a messy ponytail and bright, inquisitive eyes the color of dark chocolate. Like several of the current Cooper Security operatives, she had once worked for the government, spending six years in the FBI. If Evie wasn't mistaken, her time there had overlapped some of Isabel's and Ben Scanlon's years at the bureau, although she was pretty sure they'd been in different sections.

"We held our position until we realized they were staking out the hotel, as well." Terry Allen continued where Delilah had left off. "And we knew the Kingsleys had plans to visit the beach that morning, so—"

"How exactly did you know that?" Rita asked, not hiding her annoyance.

Delilah just smiled. "It's our job to know."

"We've been on a plane since ten-thirty Barcelona time," Andrew said in a calm, even tone of voice. Evie suspected his constant air of reasonability was a big part of his charm for her sister. How she'd ever thought she could live with a complicated man like Jesse Cooper, Evie didn't know.

But opposites often attracted, she supposed.

"Why don't we find somewhere for you to bunk

down?" Jesse suggested. He looked at his sister. "How's the decrypting coming?"

"It's coming," Shannon answered, sounding distracted.

"We have a dormitory here at Cooper Security. It's not quite a hotel, but the beds are comfortable and we can arrange a nice hot meal and a shower for you. Then you can bunk down until we can find you a safe house."

"Damn it, Jesse, I don't want to be stashed away in one of your little vaults like I'm a painting or a piece of jewelry." Rita's blue eyes flashed with temper. "Or is that the whole point of sending your goons to stake us out?" She looked at Delilah with suspicion. "I bet you never saw one of those SS whatevers you said you saw—"

Delilah just shot her a look of irritation.

"Rita, Delilah and Terry are professionals," Evie began.

Rita whirled to look at her. "What the hell did you do to your hair?"

"Cut it and dyed it so the people who tried to kidnap me twice wouldn't easily find me again," she answered flatly, annoyed with her sister's bad attitude. She tried to tell herself that Rita was exhausted and probably a lot more afraid than she was willing to admit, but there was no excuse for insulting the people who'd put their own lives on the line to keep her safe.

"Maybe we should just go with Mr. Cooper," Andrew suggested.

"Oh, go ahead and call him Jesse," Rita drawled. "You know everything there is to know about him by now."

Evie looked at Jesse for his reaction, but his face was an expressionless mask. She'd seen him shut down that way while dealing with demanding clients, but she'd also seen his expression shuttered when someone mentioned his breakup with Rita, so there was no way to know what he was really thinking. She could only guess, and right now all her guesses made her stomach tie up in knots.

"I'll take them to the dorms," she offered aloud.

"I'll come with you," Jesse said. "I don't want anyone to go anywhere in this building without backup."

"I haven't agreed to stay here," Rita snapped.

"We're staying here, at least for tonight." Andrew put his hand on her back. "I know you're tired. I'm tired, too. But at the very least, the multiple kidnapping attempts on your sister should give us pause. I wasn't sure we should have gone to Barcelona in the first place, given the situation."

"You're the one who said we should go," Rita protested.

"Your father told me I should get you out of the country."

"That's not far enough," Jesse said quietly.

Rita's gaze flew up to his face, but she bit back

whatever she had been about to say. She looked away from him quickly.

"Let's get you two a place to stay." Jesse nodded for them to follow him out of the conference room.

The walk back to the dormitory was awkward, the silence that fell among the four of them thick with tension. When Evie could take no more, she spoke just to end the silence. "How was Barcelona?"

"Lovely until a couple of relentless people with guns told us to pack our bags and bug out in half an hour," Rita answered drily.

"Did you have time to shop for souvenirs?" Evie kept her voice deliberately flippant.

Rita stopped in the middle of the hallway and turned to look at her, a smile flirting with her lips. "Mercenary brat."

Evie grinned. "Because I didn't get a chance to catch the bouquet at the reception, I figure I should get something out of this whole wedding thing."

Rita gave her a swift, fierce hug. "I worried about you the whole time."

Evie arched an eyebrow. "The whole time?"

"Most of the time," Rita answered with a blush.

Jesse stopped at a room about halfway down the hall. It took a second for Evie to realize he was putting Rita and Andrew in a room across the corridor from Evie's temporary abode. Which also put them across from the room where Jesse was staying.

Stop, Evie. Stop making yourself crazy.

Andrew dumped their luggage on the bed and sighed with relief. "I could use a shower. Do you want to go first, sweetheart?"

Rita shook her head. "Go ahead. I'll talk to Evie and Jesse out here in the hallway so you can have some privacy."

"We can go to my room," Evie suggested as they stepped out into the corridor again.

Rita ignored the suggestion, turning to Jesse with flashing blue eyes. "Is all this about what happened with us? Is this your way of punishing me for giving up on you ten years ago?"

For a second, Jesse's neutral mask slipped, and Evie saw a flash of indignation in his dark eyes. "Not everything is about you, Rita."

"Isn't it? You practically stalked my wedding. You've dragged my sister God knows where and sent your spies to ruin my honeymoon—"

"Rita, your sister was kidnapped once, almost twice, and witnessed her bodyguard's murder. In D.C. we were shot at and witnessed the gruesome death of a couple of SSU thugs."

"The SSU again." Rita grimaced.

Jesse turned away from her, his mouth a thin, tight line. "Go back into your room and get some rest. We don't know what the next few days are going to bring for us all." He crossed to his room, unlocked the door and shut it firmly behind him.

Evie stared at the closed door. He hadn't even addressed her, hadn't said good-night or suggested she get into her room and lock the door behind her. She blinked back the tears stinging her eyes and turned to her sister.

Rita was staring at Jesse's door as well, her cheeks bright with angry color. "He's always been such an arrogant control freak."

"He's trying to keep everyone safe," Evie defended. "That's a lot of responsibility."

Rita looked at Evie, her brow furrowed. "Do you think he still has feelings for me?"

Evie's gut tightened. "I don't think you stop loving someone that easily. You still love him, don't you?"

Rita's eyes softened. "Of course. But not how I love Andrew. Not anymore. You know that."

Jesse was right, Evie thought. Just the fact that she was Rita's sister complicated everything between the two of them, and all the runaway desire they might feel for each other wouldn't make those complications go away.

Rita touched Evie's chopped-off hair. "Now that I'm starting to get used to it, your hair is pretty cute like that. I even like the color. It's good with your fair skin." She held out her arms, and Evie stepped into her embrace, holding her sister tight for a moment.

"I'm glad you're home safe," she murmured. "I hope the honeymoon wasn't a complete bust."

Rita laughed. "Not a complete one, no. I'm not sure we'd have been able to have a really good honeymoon not knowing where you were or if you were okay." She let Evie go. "I'm going to go see if Andrew's out of the shower. I'd like to wash off all the travel grit myself."

"Get some sleep. We'll talk in the morning."

She waited until Rita closed the door behind her before she turned toward her room. But as she reached for the door handle, Jesse's door opened and he strode into the hall.

He stopped short when he spotted Evie. "I thought you'd gone to bed."

"I was heading that way. You going back to the conference room?"

He nodded. "I can't sleep."

"I'm going to give it a try," she said, although she doubted she'd be doing much sleeping, even as tired as she was.

The sparks flying between Jesse and her sister moments earlier had made her chest ache. Had those sparks been the natural result of spirited conflict? Or was there a lingering, underlying sexual passion that neither of them would ever get over?

And if that was the reality, what chance did Evie have of making Jesse realize that she was the Marsh sister he really belonged with?

It FELT STRANGE not having Evie by his side, Jesse realized as he crossed the bridge to the main office building. She'd been with him constantly for days now, rarely leaving his presence for more than a few minutes at a time.

He missed her.

His sister Shannon and Gideon Stone were the only people left in the conference room when he entered. "Where are the Marshes?"

"Izzy and Ben took them to the dorms not long after you and the others left. They're giving them the eastern corner suite because it's bigger. They'll be more comfortable there."

"Good idea." Jesse pulled up a chair and sat beside his sister, looking over her shoulder. The gibberish on the computer screen meant nothing to him. "Anything yet?"

"We're into the memory card now. You're looking at the code key itself. I'm just working through the pattern so that I can apply it to the journal."

"You're still missing General Marsh's part of the code."

"I know." Shannon slanted a quick look at him. "Any chance you can talk him into spilling it?"

"I doubt I'd have much chance," he admitted. "But maybe Evie will."

"You don't think Rita would do it?"

"Rita's too busy worrying about her own issues." He dismissed the idea with a wave of his hand, still feeling irritated at her earlier self-centered attitude. He didn't remember her being so spoiled, but maybe that had been their problem in the end. She wanted things her own way, and bending to someone else's will, even partially, had never been something she was willing to do for long.

She'd wanted him to quit the Marine Corps and get a desk job, complete with suit and tie. She hadn't understood how much the Marine Corps had given him a sense of purpose, a feeling of being part of something bigger than himself. Being part of something important, something that mattered. She'd wanted him to throw all that away for her, and she hadn't been willing to listen to his side of things at all. And even then, he'd loved her enough to be tempted to do what she wanted.

It had been Evie, he remembered with a faint smile, who had convinced him to stand his ground. She hadn't known anything about her sister's ultimatum, as far as he knew. At seventeen, she was involved in her own teenage drama, worrying about whether she'd be asked to the prom or whether her grades and tests scores would be good enough to get her into the college she wanted to attend.

He wasn't sure why he'd asked her, of all people, whether she thought he was being selfish for wanting to stay in the Marine Corps.

"Selfish would be walking away from your team," she'd answered thoughtfully. "You all depend on each other, right? And you're about to be deployed to Kaziristan—it would be a terrible time to leave them."

She'd been right. He'd known it, bone-deep. He'd

just needed someone to say it aloud, to reassure him that he'd made the right decision.

"Okay, I have it," Shannon announced. She stifled a yawn behind her hand. "If you want me to try to decrypt the journal tonight, though, somebody better brew a pot of coffee."

"Does it have to be tonight?" Gideon asked.

Jesse shot him a look of surprise. Gideon was usually one of his most gung ho operatives, ready to get to work in a heartbeat. But he was looking with concern at Shannon, his expression so tender it made Jesse's teeth hurt.

He swallowed a sigh. Clearly, Stone wasn't going away. Jesse was just going to have to deal with the idea of his baby sister in love with a big ol' jarhead lunk. "Shan, want to get some rest and start again in the morning?"

Her brow furrowed. "If I try to sleep now, I'll just worry at it all night anyway. But we really need General Marsh's part of the code."

"I'll see what I can do," Jesse said.

JESSE FOUND MRS. MARSH alone in the corner suite. She blinked at him with sleepy blue eyes that reminded him strongly of Evie. "He got a call from Evie and went upstairs to talk to her."

"Oh. Thanks. Sorry for waking you."

Donna Marsh caught his arm as he started to go. "Thank *you*."

He paused, surprise. "For what?"

"For protecting us. All of us. Bax won't say it, but he feels it, too."

Jesse couldn't imagine Rita's father having any sort of positive feelings toward him after all that had happened, but he managed a smile. "Try to sleep, Mrs. Marsh. Everybody's safe now."

She smiled at him and closed the door, leaving him alone in the hall.

He headed up to Evie's room, not sure what to do next. If he knew Evie as well as he thought he did, she'd be trying to convince her father to give up his part of the code. So the question was, should he let her work her magic on her father alone, or would it help to have a partner in her efforts?

It might, he conceded, but not if he was the partner in question. The mere sight of Jesse seemed to put the general's defenses up, like a porcupine confronted with an enemy.

He stopped short of Evie's door, listening, instead, at the door of the room Rita and her husband shared. They were still awake; he could hear them talking quietly beyond the closed door.

He leaned closer, trying to decide whether to knock and ask Rita to help Evie convince her father to give up his secrets. But before he could lift his hand, the door behind him opened.

He jerked away from Rita's door and turned to face Evie and her father.

"What are you doing?" Baxter Marsh asked, his expression thunderous.

"Just wondering if Rita and Andrew were still up," he answered honestly, glancing at Evie. She gazed back, her expression as dark and pained as a bruise.

Dismay coiled like a snake in his gut as he realized what they both must think of his lurking outside Rita's room. "Mrs. Marsh said Evie had called you to come see her."

The general glared back at him. "You woke my wife?"

Jesse swallowed a grimace. He couldn't win with Baxter Marsh. "Shannon has worked out General Ross's code. We already have Emmett Harlowe's code key—"

"So you need my part of the code," Marsh finished for him. He exchanged a long look with his daughter. "Evie has been telling me what information your company has gleaned about the Espera Group and AfterAssets. It's amazing how much your people have been able to piece together without being closer to the action."

"The former SSU agents have to be stopped," Jesse said with more overt passion than he was usually comfortable revealing. But he suspected the one thing Marsh wanted to know was just how committed Jesse was to following the clues wherever they led him, no matter how dark or dangerous a place that might be.

He was committed. He would never have allowed his family and colleagues to risk their lives in search of the SSU and the conspiracy they were trying to uncover if he wasn't utterly convinced that letting the SSU continue their schemes unchallenged would be dangerous to individuals and nations alike.

"Too many good people have died in the service of the Espera Group's ambitions," Jesse added. "Too many more will die or lose their basic freedoms if we allow it to go on any longer."

Marsh's eyes narrowed. "Still the Marine, even without the dress blues, aren't you?"

"Once a Marine—"

"Always a Marine," Marsh finished with a slight smile.

Evie curled her hand over her father's arm. "Will you give us your part of the code, Dad? If we have it, we can find out what General Ross knew about the Espera Group and the SSU that you and General Harlowe didn't."

Marsh stared at his daughter, worry creasing his brow. Jesse didn't doubt the decision was a struggle. Marsh's part of the code was all the leverage he had left against people who'd use his family against him without blinking.

He turned to look at Jesse finally. "Okay," he said. "I'll give you the code."

Chapter Sixteen

"Genius, really." Shannon's manic grin came from too many sleepless hours, too much coffee and the giddy satisfaction of decrypting the journal they'd spent two months trying to decode. "There are six levels of code—each code has two layers." She looked at General Marsh, who sat nearby. "Did you all come up with this together?"

Evie's father smiled. "Edward was the code man. He worked it all out and doled out the layers to Emmett and me. We knew how the code could be broken, but I can't tell you how it all works together." He shot a look at Jesse. "Your sister would have been an asset to the Corps, Cooper."

"Don't give her any ideas, sir," he murmured.

"Bottom line." Rick sounded impatient. "What does it tell us?"

"A lot you've already pieced together," Gideon admitted. "But we've come across a few things we didn't know before."

"General Ross confirms that Katrina Hilliard is

involved in whatever the SSU is up to." Shannon didn't look away from the computer screen. Her eyebrows shot up suddenly. "Oh, wow."

"What?" Jesse rounded the table to look over her shoulder.

"General Ross talked to Vince."

Evie gave a start. Vince Randall, Jesse's late brother-in-law?

"We knew Vince had seen Barton Reid with an al Adar terrorist leader—Megan and Evan gleaned that from his letters to Megan." Shannon looked at her brother. "But there were a few things we couldn't figure out."

"KH," he murmured, looking across the room at Evie. "There was a letter—Megan's husband, Vince, had hidden it inside a toy he sent home for their dog, Patton," he explained, his gaze locked with hers. His expression was so intense that she felt as if they were the only people in the room. "He sent it only a couple of days before he was killed. There were some things we couldn't decipher. One was a notation about a meeting in Tablis between KH, Barton Reid and an al Adar leader."

"Katrina Hilliard knew what Barton Reid was up to." The full treachery of the president's chief aide hit Evie in a sickening wave.

Shannon looked equally queasy. "General Ross writes that Vince saw Hilliard and Reid in deep conversation with Malik Tahrim, an al Adar operative. General Ross calls him a 'very bad actor' in the region."

"He was one of the terrorists Amanda was tracking around the time al Adar grabbed her off the street of Tablis and tortured her," Rick said.

"Amanda?" Evie's father looked confused. "Who's Amanda?"

"My wife," Rick answered. "I think you were still in Kaziristan when she was working for CIA. You'd have known her as Tara Brady."

Her father's eyebrows arched. "I see."

"Did you know any of this?" Evie asked, curious.

"Not all of it. Edward was the one who spearheaded our attempts to compile the evidence. I knew MacLear was running covert operations with impunity. That was my part of the investigation—tracking their movements and figuring out if Jackson Melville knew what was going on. The Department of Defense had paid MacLear millions for troop support missions. If MacLear was abusing our trust in them, we needed to know."

"What did you learn?"

"We were still looking into that question when the SSU got caught red-handed." The general looked at Jesse. "Your cousins had something to do with how that all went down, I believe."

"What part did General Harlowe have in the investigation?" As an accountant, Evie hadn't been privy to the more confidential information that passed through Cooper Security. But she figured she had a right to know what was going on, given her own personal stake in seeing justice done where the remnants of the SSU were concerned.

"The Air Force had access to satellite images of troop movements. Harlowe's part was to get his hands on those recordings and images and piece together any anomalies," the general answered. "He was the one who first made Edward suspect the SSU were involved in his son's death." He looked at Gideon, his eyes narrowing. "Did you have any idea, Captain Stone?"

"Not until General Ross shared his suspicions," Gideon answered. "I know there were MacLear operatives working with our unit to provide transportation and troop support, but I couldn't tell you if any of them were SSU or not. We didn't mix much."

"These files don't really prove anything," Isabel commented, sounding impatient. "They give us a lot of places to look, but there's not any actual evidence here. You need evidence to get a conviction."

"What we have here may be enough to remove Katrina Hilliard from the president's cabinet," her sister Megan pointed out. "That's not nothing."

"It's not enough," Jesse said flatly. "If the generals are right about what they've compiled here, Hilliard, Barton Reid and the Espera Group have systematically used their own private army to undermine democratic reformers in several sovereign, oil-producing nations to push forward their own plans for a transnational regulatory commission to control oil production and revenue. It's heinous on every conceivable level."

"Jesse's right," Evie's father said quietly. "Removing Katrina Hilliard from office isn't enough. Convicting Barton Reid isn't enough. We have to bring down the whole damned conspiracy. Edward Ross died trying to make sure these people got the punishment they deserve."

"We've decoded the journal and we're still not any closer to making that happen?" Megan's husband, Evan Pike, sounded incredulous.

"Wait a sec," Shannon said, looking intently at the computer. "We may be closer than you think."

Jesse crossed to where she sat and looked over her shoulder at the laptop screen. "What've you got?"

"A name. Endrex."

Endrex? Evie shook her head. It couldn't be the same guy—

"Who the hell is Endrex?" Jesse's brow creased with frustration.

"General Ross refers to him as a hacker," Shannon said, "but from what he describes it sounds like he's actually a cryppie."

"A what?" Isabel asked.

"A cryptographer," Evie said before Shannon could answer. "Someone who hacks cryptography programs. Not necessarily illegally," she added quickly. "If Endrex is who I think it is, he may have done some work for the Marine Corps a few years ago."

"You know who this Endrex is?" Jesse asked.

"I knew a guy who went by that handle," she said carefully, not sure she was right. "Complete computer genius. He was at Quantico when we were stationed at the base there. I was fifteen at the time. He tried to teach me how to program, but I didn't have the instincts for it."

"Not a Marine?" her father asked.

"No, a civilian. He'd have never made it as a Marine. He wore his disdain for authority on his sleeve, but he was brilliant at code breaking."

"You sound as if you had a crush on him," Jesse murmured.

She couldn't read his masklike expression, but his tone was light enough. "Maybe a little one. I thought he was cool and transgressive—that's kind of a big deal when you're fifteen."

Jesse grinned at her then, and she gazed back at him, feeling utterly helpless against her attraction to him, no matter how certain she'd become that a relationship between them could only end badly.

"Do you know where we can find him?" Rick Cooper asked.

She dragged her gaze away from Jesse. "Physically? No. He left Quantico shortly before we did."

"But can you contact him?" Shannon asked. She patted the laptop's keyboard. "On here?"

Evie thought about it. "Maybe. He showed me

a few places on the net where he and his friends hung out."

"What was his real name?" Jesse asked.

"I don't know. He called himself Endrex, and everyone he was working with at Quantico did, too. I don't even know if he was working with the Marines or with the FBI academy. Or the Air Force Office of Special Investigations, for that matter. Lots of secret things go on in Quantico."

"I can make some calls," Ben Scanlon suggested. "I'm still on good terms with the Bureau. Agent Brand may know who Endrex is."

"And if he doesn't," Delilah Hammond added, "he'll know who to ask."

Ben glanced at the other Cooper Security agent. "You worked with Brand when you were with the Bureau?"

"Some," she answered noncommittally.

"I'll make the call," Ben said.

"Wait." Evie spoke up to be heard over the hum of discussion beginning to take over the conference room.

Everyone quieted down, turning to look at her.

"Endrex may have been working with the good guys, but the man I knew won't make it easy to find him if he doesn't want to be found," she warned. "He sees himself as an outlaw, even if he wasn't really. If he has evidence of the Espera Group's crimes, he'll know he's in danger. If you try to go through official channels, you may chase him underground."

"So what do you suggest?" Jesse asked.

"Let me try to contact him online," she said. "Like I told Shannon, I know some of the places he'd go. If I can reach him that way and regain his trust, we might be able to get him to meet us."

"If he has evidence that can bring down the Espera Group, we have to get our hands on it," Jesse said flatly. "You can't let him hold on to his cards. Understand?"

She nodded. "I can do this." Her voice came out strong and sure, far more sure than she actually felt. Her gut muscles quivered with unease as she started to feel the full impact of what she'd just agreed to do.

Endrex was wily and smarter than she could ever hope to be. He knew the internet as intimately as a lover, and there was no way she could catch him there if he decided to run.

They'd stayed in touch for a few years after he left Quantico and she and her family had relocated to Alabama, but by the time Evie was in college, life and constraints on her time had gotten in the way of their virtual friendship. They hadn't communicated in over a year, and that had been a brief, unexpected "Hi, how are you" instant message initiated by Endrex.

Thinking back, she wondered now at the timing of his message. Her father's retirement from the Marine Corps had made the news, mostly because of his high-profile involvement in later years with the politically volatile peacekeeping mission in Kaziristan. Endrex had contacted her shortly after the retirement hit the news.

Had he wanted something in particular? He'd seemed guarded, although for a guy like him, a hint of paranoia wasn't unusual.

"I'll need to go to my apartment," she told Jesse. "He'll be able to trace my location, so it's better if I'm on a computer that tracks back to me."

"I'll take you there," he said with a short nod.

"I want to go with you," her father said.

Evie smiled at him. "Dad, Jesse will protect me. You and Mom are still targets. You really need to stay here and let Cooper Security protect you."

"It's hard for a Marine to do that," he grumbled.

She crossed to give him a fierce hug. "Okay, then you stay here and protect them. I'll be back as soon as I can."

As she and Jesse left the conference room, the buzz of renewed discussion cut off abruptly with the closing of the door, leaving them alone in a silent, semidark inner corridor.

Evie's steps faltered to a halt, and she leaned against the hallway wall, her knees trembling.

Jesse moved closer, concern darkening his eyes. "Are you okay?"

"What am I doing?" she asked. "I'm not a secret

agent. I just made everybody in there think I know what I'm doing."

His brow furrowed. "And you don't?"

"I don't know." She covered her face with her hands. "I didn't lie about knowing Endrex. And I do think he'll talk to me. But you all think I can make him turn over the evidence to you just because I mooned over him when I was fifteen and he indulged me, and I don't know if I can."

Jesse gently pulled her hands away from her face and tilted her chin up, forcing her to look at him. "Everybody in there knows you'll do your best. That's all you can do. Do you think we don't screw up sometimes? You know we do. I blew the surveillance of Gamble back in D.C. I should have known there was a possibility we'd run into the guys who kidnapped you. I mean, we went to D.C. to find out who'd sent them, so I should have known there was a chance Gamble would be meeting with them instead of his girlfriend. We were too exposed. I never should have let that happen."

"You couldn't plan for every possibility," she protested, closing her hands over his where they rested on her shoulders.

"I should have planned better," he argued. "But my point is, we know you'll do the best you can. That's all we could possibly ask of you." He tugged one hand free from hers and brushed a lock of hair out of her face. "You've already gone so far beyond the call of your duties here, I don't know whether to sack you or give you a bloody promotion."

"How about you just hold me a minute?" she whispered, her heart squeezing into a painful knot. She hated herself for being so needy, so unable to distance herself from him once and for all. But she couldn't regret it when he wrapped her in his arms, molding her body against his until she felt as if she was irrevocably a part of him.

The tearing sensation when he finally let her go was more painful than she'd anticipated.

"Let's get out of here." Flattening his hand against the small of her back, he guided her toward the underground parking garage where Cooper Security kept its fleet of company vehicles.

It had been a long time since he'd thought of himself as Nolan Cavanaugh. That was a normal name. A little upper-crust. A better name for his real-estate-mogul father and his day-trader brother than a guy like him.

He was Endrex. Single name, like Cher or Elvis. In his neck of cyberspace, he was bigger than either.

He used to get a kick out of the notoriety, especially when he thought about how appalled his father would be at the idea. His son the subculture net head. The old man had never understood him. Never really tried.

It had been years since they'd spoken, although he kept track of his family on the net. Checked

Drake's emails now and then to make sure he wasn't gambling away his fortune. Tapped into his father's business to make sure everything was going well. His parents were still together—he knew that much because he'd recently listened in on the email conversation between his brother and his mother regarding his parents' fortieth-anniversary party at the country club in November.

Good for the old folks. That kind of commitment was rare in the world these days.

Dawn was a rosy hint in the window across the room, a reminder that he hadn't slept at all the night before. He never got close to the windows these days. Way too risky considering what all had been going down for the past few months.

He'd been smart. Taken precautions and prepared for this day. He'd known it was coming.

Breakfast would be dry cereal and milk he'd made from powder. Lunch would be something out of a can. So would dinner. He'd streamlined his life to the basics since he'd read the news about Edward Ross's death online a few months ago.

He wondered if the other two generals had any idea who he was. General Ross had promised to keep his existence their little secret, but the general had been establishment to the core. People like him weren't nearly as good at keeping secrets as they thought they were.

He'd taken the place in Birmingham because it was safely anonymous. He didn't stick out much here in Southside, among the artsy iconoclasts and sloppy college crowd. Nobody gave him a second look. And even the people who'd heard of Endrex couldn't have picked him out from a crowd.

He should get some shut-eye, but he couldn't shake the feeling he needed to stay awake. He'd been taking some chances over the past few days, sniffing around some areas of the net where he might not be the biggest, baddest dog on the block. It was a chance he'd felt he had to take after the mercs had gone after Marsh's youngest daughter. He needed to know if anyone out there knew who he was or what he had in his possession.

He hadn't turned it over to anyone yet. General Ross had agreed with him that it was too soon. Even the old soldier hadn't known who the good guys and bad guys were. That's what he'd been working on when the bastards got him.

So Endrex was still sitting on the files he'd stolen off a handful of government networks. Really, the idiots should have better info security these days. The Chinese would never put up with this kind of crummy security, but they'd sure as hell exploit it.

He wondered if there were Chicom agents out there with their hands on the same stuff he'd found. He wondered what they were doing with it, who they were putting pressure on right this very minute.

A pinging noise drew his attention back to his computer screen. Someone had just entered an old chat area he hadn't visited in years. It had fallen into disuse after some cracker idiot tried to use the room for an illegal bank hack. The feds had swarmed the place and run off all the legit hacks. He didn't know who'd have stumbled into that place again after all this time.

Curiosity nudged at him, and he pulled up that program. There was a lone screen moniker listed in the user box. Leatherbrat.

He released a huff of disbelief. Little Evie Marsh? After all this time?

Or was it a trick?

Text popped up in the chat area. Long time no type.

His lips curved. Little dork. Couldn't even come up with an original opener. But his smile faded quickly. It could be a trick. Her father had said he didn't know where she was, although the police view was that she'd disappeared under her own steam.

But what if they were wrong? What if she was with her captors right now and somehow they'd learned about him?

What if they were using her to smoke him out?

Chapter Seventeen

"He's just sitting there." Jesse was growing impatient as they waited for Endrex to answer her overture. "Are you even sure it's really him? Couldn't anyone call himself Endrex?"

"He wouldn't put up with identity theft for long, and anyone with half a brain and even passing knowledge of the hacker world would know the kinds of things Endrex could do to their lives without even breaking a sweat."

Text popped up on the screen suddenly.

Safe word.

"Safe word?" Jesse asked aloud, his gaze snapping away from the screen to search hers.

She laughed, her eyes widening. "Not that kind of safe word. He's asking for verification that I'm who I say I am."

"You barely said anything at all."

"He'll recognize the screen name. He's the one who gave it to me."

"Leatherbrat?"

"Leatherneck's Brat."

"Well, yeah, I figured that—"

She just smiled at him and typed in a word. Snickerdoodle.

Jesse leaned closer, laying his hands on her shoulders. As her muscles trembled beneath his fingers, he tamped down a surge of raw male triumph at her feminine reaction to his touch.

When this was all over, he and Evie Marsh were going to have to have a long, serious talk about what was happening between them. Work through all the obstacles between them that she seemed to think were immovable. Because there was no way he was going to let her walk out of his life the way Rita had. He'd make any sacrifice, give in to any demand she might have, to keep her around.

His hands trembled as the full meaning of his thoughts hit him like a brick bat. He'd never been willing to make those concessions for Rita. All she'd asked of him was to find a different job, and he couldn't do it. But if Evie asked him to sell his shares of Cooper Security and follow her across the globe doing charity work, he'd do it without hesitation, just to be with her.

Oh, my God, he thought. *I love her. I really love her.*

"Here we go," Evie said.

Jesse looked at the laptop. Words had popped onto the screen. Are you okay? Heard about your ordeal. "Which ordeal?" he asked. "The attempted kidnappings or the accident in D.C.?"

"Not sure," she answered. Her fingers flew across the keyboard, her answer appearing on the screen. I'm fine, but I need to see you. In person. Where are you now?

A few seconds later, Endrex typed back, Closer than you think.

"Does he know where you're living now?" Jesse asked.

"Yeah, I talked to him briefly a while back and mentioned I'd moved here permanently." Evie typed in a new message. Tell me where to find you and I'll come to you. We need to talk.

"How do you think he'll respond to that?" Jesse murmured, pulling up a chair before his shaking knees betrayed him.

"I don't know. He tends to paranoia."

The wait for an answer seemed interminable. When it finally came, it was brief. They're here. Can't talk.

"What?" Jesse asked.

Who's there? Evie typed in.

Come visit came the response. Look for the Storyteller. Noon.

"Who the hell is the Storyteller?" Jesse asked.

"I don't know. She typed in a request for more information, but Endrex's name disappeared from the chat list. "I think he's gone."

"How paranoid is this guy? Paranoid enough to imagine people are after him when they're not?"

"Possibly. But if General Ross's journal was right and Endrex has actual evidence that could bring down the Espera Group, do you think they'd hesitate for a moment to try to take him out?"

"But how would they know he has it? As far as we know, the only record of that is the general's journal, and we only just now deciphered the code. Even if we had a mole standing right there in the room with us this morning, there hasn't been enough time for anyone to figure out who he really is and how to find him."

"I don't know," Evie said, looking worried. "I have a really bad feeling about this. What if someone's found him? They might be taking him captive right now and torturing him to find out what he has on them."

Jesse hoped not. If the SSU got the information from Endrex that they wanted, they wouldn't leave him alive. Their best hope to bring down the Espera Group would be gone.

"He said he was closer than I thought. Could he be in Alabama?"

"I don't know." Frustration drove him to his feet, and he started pacing the floor of her small living room, trying to focus his mind on nothing but the question of where to find Endrex. But focus was hard to come by when he was surrounded by Evie's light, fresh fragrance. The apartment seemed to be permeated by the scent. "If he was here in the state, where would he settle? Did he have any connections here?"

"Not that I know of, but I didn't know very much about his personal life. I don't even know his real name. My dad might be able to find out."

Definitely a place to start, Jesse thought, pulling out his cell phone. He got his sister Megan on the line. "Megan, I need to talk to General Marsh. Is he anywhere around?"

"Sure, he's right here." Megan passed the phone to the general.

"Have you learned something?" Marsh asked gruffly, skipping the greetings.

"We're not sure. Evie doesn't know Endrex's real name. Do you have any contacts who might have known his given name? It would help us track him down much more quickly."

"Sure, I can make a call or two."

"Thank you, sir. Call me back when you have it." Jesse hung up and turned back to Evie, who sat tense and hunched at the computer as she scrolled through search-engine results. The screen changed, bringing up a page with a large photo of a fountain in the middle.

She straightened suddenly and twisted to look at him. "Look at this."

He sat beside her again and looked at the computer screen. The photo that filled the screen featured a fountain in Birmingham, Alabama. Inside the fountain, a bronze statue of a man with a ram's head was reading a book to an assortment of animals situated on bronze circles, while bronze frogs shot streams of water from their mouths.

The caption under the picture read, "The Storyteller, a bronze sculpture by artist Frank Fleming, sits in the fountain in Five Points South."

"The Storyteller," Evie murmured, her eyes wide with excitement.

"WHAT IF IT'S THE OTHER Storyteller?"

Evie looked away from the fountain visible across Magnolia Avenue and met Jesse's dark gaze. "The other one was in Buckhead outside Atlanta. Definitely not an Endrex sort of place."

"And Five Points South is?"

"Absolutely." She ticked off the reasons. "Artsy, bohemian, popular with the college crowd, has a thriving slacker-chic underground—"

"And?"

"He'd want to blend in. His notoriety was all in cyberspace. In the normal world, he'd want to stay as low-key as possible. Not attract attention."

He didn't answer, just stared back at her through those dark, mysterious eyes that made her stomach tighten and her heart race.

He hadn't wanted her to come with him to Birmingham, but she'd made him see the need. Endrex knew her. He'd trusted her enough to give her a clue where to find him.

Even with Jesse stopping at the office to pick up extra weapons and ammo and brief the others on their plans, they'd reached Birmingham well before noon. After driving around Five Points South a couple of times to scope out the area, they'd parked in the back lot of a restaurant near the Storyteller fountain on Highland Avenue. The mid-October weather was still mild, warm enough to lure a handful of patrons onto the outdoor patio across the street from the fountain. Jesse and Evie had joined them, ordering from the brunch menu.

Evie wasn't hungry, even though she'd skipped breakfast. Too much nervous energy, she supposed. But she tried to eat a little of the cheese omelet Jesse had coaxed her to order as she kept an eye on the fountain.

"Are you sure you'll recognize him?" Jesse asked quietly.

"I don't know. It's been eleven years." He had been in his early twenties when she'd known him back in Virginia. In a decade he could have added weight. Started to lose his hair or go gray. For all she knew, he'd gone establishment, at least on the outside. Suit, tie, haircut and all. Had she been crazy to convince Jesse to rush down to Birmingham to meet a man she hadn't seen in years who could be hundreds of miles from here?

Ten o'clock ticked over to eleven, and the waiter started to eye them resentfully. Jesse ordered another orange juice for each of them, buying them a little extra patience from the server.

"What if they've captured him?" she asked quietly, her stomach in knots. "Or worse? Maybe I should go wait by the fountain."

His mouth tightened. "By yourself?"

"You'd spook him off."

She could tell by the look in his dark eyes that he knew she was right—and didn't like it one bit. "Okay," he said, reluctance oozing from his voice. "But the second anything gets the least bit hinky—"

"I'll get out of there," she promised.

She felt his gaze burning into her back as she crossed Magnolia Avenue to reach the fountain. The splash of water on stone and bronze muted some of the traffic sounds of the busy five-point intersection, but it also made listening for any approaching footsteps next to impossible.

With the time beginning to approach midday, foot traffic had picked up as people from nearby businesses took advantage of the warm day to walk to area restaurants for an early lunch hour. Evie eyed each passing person as she pretended to study the fountain artwork.

There were men and women dressed in a rainbow array of medical scrubs, probably lunchtime escapees from the two hospitals in the Southside area. Men in formal business suits rubbed elbows with twentysomethings in sloppy plaids and jeans. Women in jewel-colored power suits, older teens in jeans and belly-ring-baring T-shirts, men in golf shirts and khakis—the variety was overwhelming.

And somewhere in this crowd of kinetic humanity, she was supposed to be able to pick out a man she hadn't seen in over ten years?

She looked across the street, locking gazes with Jesse. He was on the phone but he didn't take his eyes off her. Tension lined his face and thinned his mouth to a tight line as he watched from afar.

Suddenly his brow furrowed and he leaned forward, his muscles bunching as if he were ready to launch himself across the street.

From behind, a hand closed around her shoulder, making her jump. She whirled around, ready to fight, but the clear green eyes that met hers hadn't changed a bit in ten years.

"Leatherbrat? Love the red hair."

She started to relax, until she realized the smile in Endrex's green eyes belied the tension his lean body betrayed in every taut tendon and nervous twitch. He hadn't changed much in the time they'd been apart; he was still thin, loose-limbed and hungry-looking. He dressed a little more neatly, his sandy hair brushed back into a ponytail and his shirt a button-up rather than the faded graphic T-shirts he'd preferred when he was working in Virginia.

"You said to meet you," she said carefully, not sure whether she'd misread his urgency.

"I can't believe you actually came." His words

came out in a jittery laugh as he gestured at the fountain. "I didn't give you much to go on."

"Either here or Buckhead," she said with a smile. "You're not the Buckhead type."

"Can we get out of here? It's a little open for my tastes." His gaze darted around, clearly looking for something.

"Are you in some kind of trouble?"

"Always, Leatherbrat."

"You can call me Evie." She shot him a curious glance. "Do you have a name or are we just going with Endrex?"

He looked back at her, his eyes slightly narrowed. It took him a moment to respond, but he finally answered, "Call me Cav."

"Okay, Cav." She wished she dared look back at Jesse, but Cav was so wired that she was afraid any wrong move on her part would spook him away and they'd never be able to find him again. "Where do you want to go?"

"My bike's over here." He nodded toward the line of vehicles parked along Magnolia Avenue. She spotted a motorcycle parked about ten parking slots down from the intersection. "I brought an extra helmet just for you."

Now the urge to look back at Jesse was overwhelming. He would be furious if she got on the motorcycle with Endrex—Cav—and rode away without letting him know where they were headed, even with the precautions they'd taken. And he'd be justified.

But she needed to know whether General Ross was right. Did Cav have evidence that could bring down the Espera Group and put an end to their crimes? He was the only person who could answer that question, and thanks to their former friendship, he might be willing to tell her everything he knew. Maybe even hand over the evidence to her and Jesse for safekeeping.

It was a risk she was going to have to take.

"Are you in danger?" she asked before she gave Cav a final answer.

"Like you wouldn't believe. So are you." He met her gaze without flinching. "You're not surprised, are you?"

She shook her head. "I figured that out a few days ago when someone grabbed me at my sister's wedding and threw me in the back of a truck."

"After all that, I can't believe you came here alone." He leaned closer. "Why did you?"

She almost told him about Jesse then. But he looked like a skittish colt ready to bolt at the first provocation, so she kept the truth about Jesse's presence quiet. "I want to know what you have that can bring down the Espera Group."

His eyes widened. "How much do you know?"

"Enough to know they have to be stopped." She lowered her voice to a near whisper. "I know they've been killing people and manipulating foreign governments to clear the path for their plans."

"Their hired goons are here, you know."

"That's what you said."

"They've probably gone through my room by now. I got out before they spotted me." He laughed nervously. "At least, I hope I did."

"You can't go back there."

He shrugged. "I don't keep the important stuff there anyway. Just a laptop they can have, for all I care." He patted the messenger bag draped around his neck and shoulder. "I have what I need here."

"What about the evidence?"

His eyes narrowed. "That's somewhere safe." Cav gave her a slight nudge toward the motorcycle and followed as she started walking in that direction.

What would Jesse do now? she wondered. He had to be on the verge of chasing them down and making a scene to keep her from going with Cav.

Please, Jesse. Please don't do it.

Whether he liked it or not, she had to do this her way.

JESSE THREW A TWENTY on the table to pay for their food and the tip, keeping his eye on Evie and her companion. He'd hoped this situation wouldn't transpire, even as he'd prepared for the possibility. Short of leaving her behind, he couldn't have prevented her from doing what she believed was necessary to get the evidence General Ross had died trying to protect.

And even leaving her behind would have been a temporary fix at best. She'd made bringing down these conspirators her mission the second she realized the implications of letting the Espera Group get away with their plans. She wasn't the sort of woman who could sit back and watch a disaster unfold if she thought she could help stop it.

That trait was one of the many things he had come to love about her, even if it scared him out of his mind.

Evie and the man Jesse assumed must be Endrex stopped at a motorcycle just as he reached the parking lot. Endrex handed her a helmet, spurring Jesse to move faster before he lost them. He'd been forced to park at the farthest end of the lot, where there was no good view of the street, so there was nearly a minute where Evie was completely out of his sight. Hurrying, he backed the car out of the parking slip and headed for the Magnolia Avenue exit, scanning the street to see how far they'd gotten.

The motorcycle was sitting in the same place he'd last seen it. The helmet Endrex had handed to Evie sat on the motorcycle seat.

But Evie and Endrex were nowhere around.

Struggling to quell the first gush of panic pouring into his gut, Jesse turned onto Magnolia Avenue and followed the road to the five-point intersection, scanning the converging streets for any sign of Evie and her friend on foot. But there was nothing. No sign of them anywhere.

Circling back, he drove back up Magnolia Avenue past the motorcycle again without seeing either of them. After another couple of circuits, he pulled into an empty parking slot and checked his cell phone. No messages, no texts, no missed calls.

Damn it, Evie, where did you go? This wasn't part of our agreement.

He accessed the company's GPS locator application and typed in the code of the tracker he'd given Evie before they left Chickasaw County that morning. Hitting Enter, he waited, breathless, for a signal.

There. A bright red flashing dot appeared on the small map, moving fast. She was in a vehicle, he realized, heading north up 20th Street toward Birmingham's downtown district.

Jesse's gut coiled into a hot, tight knot.

Chapter Eighteen

"Was this a setup?" Evie kept her voice low, acutely aware of the two men sitting in the front of the panel van. She and Cav sat in the back, their hands cuffed to a pair of hooks bolted to the side of the van.

"I wish." He looked authentically terrified, she noted. He had every right to be because the two men who'd shoved gun barrels into their backs and hustled them into the panel van hadn't been playing around.

"Make one stupid move and you're both dead," the taller man had told them as he cuffed them into the windowless belly of the dark green van. Dark-haired and dark-eyed, he was built like a tank, with massive shoulders and arms the size of tree limbs. His companion, the driver, was smaller and less brutishly muscular, although he looked as if he'd hold his own in a fight. He had sandy hair and very pale eyes, striking in his tanned face.

Both men had *professional* written all over them,

which almost certainly meant they were SSU thugs of some ilk.

"Have you ever seen either of these guys before?" she asked quietly.

Cav shrugged, his cuffs clanking, drawing a warning look from the dark-haired man.

Panic bloomed like a poisonous flower in Evie's gut, threatening to swamp her with full-blown terror. She couldn't let that happen. If she wanted to get herself and Cav out of this mess, keeping her head was vital.

They weren't alone at least. Jesse was out there somewhere, and she knew, bone-deep, that he'd never stop looking for her until he found her. As long as the GPS tracker in her earring was working, Jesse would be able to track her location. The captors had taken the Ruger from her holster but hadn't searched her for any other weapons, so they hadn't found the slim, multibladed knife tucked in the bottom of her bra, beneath her right breast.

She hoped they wouldn't search her again.

"What they're looking for—" Evie paused, eyeing their captors. Neither man seemed to be paying attention to them. She lowered her voice further. "Do you have it on you?"

He gave an almost imperceptible shake of his head. She wasn't sure if it was a yes or a no.

She tried to figure out where they were going, but all she could see was what was visible through the van's windshield. And their captors blocked most of that view. Still, she got the sense that they were moving away from the business district into a residential area by the way the trees lining the road ahead dappled the light coming into the van.

Logic told her their captors would want to stash her and Cav somewhere private. Maybe a house or an old, abandoned building? It wouldn't matter ultimately. As long as she could keep her earrings in her ears, Jesse should have a chance to find her.

The van finally pulled to a stop, and the engine cut out, filling the vehicle with oppressive silence. The big man with dark hair turned to look at them, his expression hard. "If I hear a peep out of either one of you, both of you are dead. Understand?"

Evie suspected he was bluffing—the SSU and the people they worked for needed to get their hands on the evidence Cav was hiding, and it would be almost impossible to do if he were dead. But she didn't try testing her theory. Their situation was dire but not desperate enough to warrant a suicide mission yet.

The burly man unlocked Evie's cuffs first, hauling her bodily out of the van before his accomplice opened the cuffs around Cav's wrists. His arm wrapped around her waist as he half walked, half carried her around a shaggy crape myrtle bush that filled her view. When they cleared the edge of the bush, she got a quick look at where they were going as the man shoved her up a shallow pair of steps into a screened-in side porch.

Their would-be jail was an old two-story house with flaking gray paint that once might have been white. Tall crape myrtle bushes draped with aggressive kudzu vines blocked the house from most of the neighboring homes around the property. She could barely make out glimpses of the faded siding through the thick leaves and vines.

She decided not to struggle, as she had no way of knowing if there were people in the nearby houses who might hear her calls for help. Safer, for the moment, to let the situation play out according to her captors' plans. If these men behaved true to SSU form, they planned to use her as leverage against Cav to get him to tell them what they wanted to know. They had no way of knowing that Jesse could find her with the flick of a button on his cell phone.

The next few hours might be horribly unpleasant, but she would almost certainly survive them. All she needed to do was to keep her head long enough for Jesse to locate her.

The side porch door led into a shabby kitchen not much bigger than the one in Evie's small apartment. The place smelled of mildew and stale cigarettes, and the urge to sneeze tickled her nose. "What is this place?" she asked. It must have been a home once. Had the SSU bought the property or just taken it over like squatters?

The man's answer was to shove her down a dark corridor to the far side of the house. He stopped in front of a small door, opening it to reveal a walk-in linen closet lined on either side with shelves. No windows and only the one door in or out.

The burly man pushed her through the narrow center aisle of the closet and into a rickety metal folding chair at the back of the closet. He grabbed both of her wrists in one large fist and fished a set of flex cuffs out of his pocket. Evie almost made the mistake of smiling, but she held it in, trying to infuse her expression with the appropriate amount of terror. It wasn't hard—for all the hope she was holding out that Jesse would find her soon, she knew she could be in grave danger.

But at least she'd be cuffed with plastic with her hands in front of her where she could easily get to the knife hidden in her bra.

"Make noise and your friend will regret it. Understand?" The big man locked the door behind her, pitching the room into utter darkness.

She heard the ragged sound of her own breathing in the close, silent room and realized for all her trust in Jesse to find her, she was still scared witless. She'd never liked close quarters, and she particularly hated them in the dark.

Okay, Marsh. Get ahold of yourself. She breathed evenly, trying not to let the tickle in her nose send her into a sneezing fit. She needed to stay calm, keep her head.

Only two things you have to do, she told herself silently, easing her hands under her bra to slip the knife into her palm. *Stay alert and get ready to make your move whenever the opportunity arises.*

She could do it, she thought, squaring her shoulders and lifting her chin against the smothering dark.

She'd been trained by the best.

THE TRACKING BEACON had led Jesse on a winding tour of north Birmingham, past the civic center and eastward toward the Red Mountain Expressway before the beacon came to a permanent stop.

Wherever Evie was going, she'd arrived.

On a detailed mapping program, he narrowed her location to a street about five blocks from where he currently was. He took a chance and made a quick drive down the street in question, taking in the surroundings as quickly and nonchalantly as he could.

There were five houses in a row on a narrow street, sitting relatively close to each other, their yards grown over with weeds, unpruned bushes and a generous infestation of kudzu vines that had grown up over bushes, fences and trees alike. The general unkempt state of the properties served to isolate them from each other, blocking views and no doubt discouraging any neighborly forays onto adjacent properties.

Evie had to be in one of them, but the tracker couldn't pinpoint exactly which one. And if Evie was there against her will, choosing the wrong one could be a disaster, tipping off her captors that she had backup. There was no telling what kind of danger that knowledge would put her in.

Despite the impatient fear gnawing at his gut, he parked at the far end of the alley behind the row of houses and made a phone call, summoning every ounce of control he had. After a few transfers, he finally reached his target, Birmingham police detective Briggs Cooper, his uncle Jay's son. Briggs's deep voice rumbled over the line. "Jesse, how the hell are you?"

"Small talk later, Briggs. I have a situation."

Two HOURS OF WAITING for something to happen had killed Evie's previous confidence. Only the faint glow of waning daylight seeping under the closet door drove back the unrelenting darkness, and if Jesse didn't find her soon, even that small bit of light would be gone.

She fought the temptation to check her watch every few seconds to relieve the gloom with the faint glow of the illuminated dial, as watching the clock seemed to make the time move that much more slowly. Was there something wrong with the tracker in her earring? She didn't dare check for fear she would drop the earring in the dark and be unable to find it again.

For the first time in over an hour, she heard a noise beyond her own breathing. A muffled cry—Cav, she realized, making out the words. "Hey!" he was calling. "Hey, guys? Are you still out there?"

She listened for a response, anxiety knotting her stomach. If these guys had wanted them dead, they'd have killed them already. But why hadn't they already started trying to use her to convince Cav to give up his evidence?

She stifled a grim chuckle. Was she actually longing for a torture session just to break up the monotony of being stuck here in the dark?

"Hey, are you even out there? We've got a problem!" Cav's voice sounded fainter than before. She thought she heard a low, choking cough. "You think I haven't taken steps to ensure that if I die, the evidence comes to light? You think I'm stupid?"

The last few words were definitely punctuated by coughs. Evie pressed her ear to the wall on the side from which Cav's voice had come. She heard more coughing.

Then she smelled it. The sulfuric odor of a gas leak.

Their captors hadn't brought them here to ask them questions at all.

They'd brought them here to die.

JESSE WATCHED FROM DOWN the street, fingers drumming on the steering wheel, as his cousin climbed the steps to the front porch of the dilapidated two-story house on the corner. It was the most overgrown of the five houses and the only one not owned by the city and scheduled for condemnation. It was owned by a company, not a person—

Audiovisual Assets LLC, according to his cousin Briggs, who'd finally called ten minutes ago with the information.

"We're pretty sure that's an SSU company," Jesse had told his cousin.

Briggs had brought a fellow detective for backup, a tall, barrel-chested mountain of a black man named Caleb Lowell. They arrived dressed in jeans and golf shirts, carrying clipboards, driving a slick Mustang Cobra nobody would mistake for an unmarked police car.

Briggs had gotten into Jesse's car to tell him what was going down, then joined Lowell on foot. They'd made a show of going to two of the uninhabited houses first, in case anyone was watching.

Now they stood on the porch of the house in question, and Powell knocked on the front door, the sound loud enough to carry all the way to where Jesse sat in his car.

After a minute without a response Lowell knocked again. He looked at Briggs, then both men glanced toward the street. Briggs gave a nod.

Jesse checked the GLOCK's magazine and double-checked the chambered round. He and Briggs had agreed that Jesse's part was simple and singular: find Evie and get her out of danger. It would be up to Briggs and his partner to take down the bad guys and get Endrex to safety.

Briggs turned to greet him as he climbed the

porch steps. "We're hearing something inside, but it doesn't sound like a voice. Since your GPS tracker shows your friend may be inside and possibly in danger, we think we can go in warrantless due to exigent circumstances."

Jesse made an impatient face. "Let's just do it."

While Powell returned to the Cobra to retrieve the battering ram Briggs had brought with them, Jesse walked down the porch and tried looking in the window, his gut twisting. Would those men have left Evie and Endrex alone here? What if the sound Briggs had heard was an animal trapped inside? What if his GPS system had gone haywire?

What if Evie was already dead?

The sound of heavy footsteps on the porch stairs made him turn, and as he did so, a whiff of odor made him freeze in place. It was a foul smell, the sulfuric stench of rotting eggs.

It came from inside the house.

Powell and Briggs already had the streamlined battering ram between them, ready to slam into the door. The first hit would stress the metal dead bolt, slide the pieces against each other.

Possibly strike sparks.

"No!" Jesse sprang forward, closing his hand over his cousin's arm. He caught Briggs in mid-swing, killing the momentum. The battering ram glanced weakly off the wooden door.

Briggs stared at Jesse as if he'd lost his mind. "What the hell, Jesse?"

"Gas," Jesse answered, his pulse roaring in his ears. "I smell gas."

IF I GET OUT OF HERE ALIVE, Evie thought, *I'm going to buy Megan a whole month of steak dinners.* Jesse's sister's knife-in-the-bra trick might be all that was standing between Evie and death.

But only if the saw attachment of this little multibladed knife could hold up to the task of sawing through two thick layers of plaster.

"Cav? You hanging in there?" For several minutes, she'd heard little from her friend but sporadic coughing.

She heard a faint sound that might have been Cav's answer. She hoped it had been. Even though the larger risk from a gas leak was ignition, inhalation could be bad enough, especially if enough gas was leaking to displace the oxygen in the air. From what she could remember about Cav from years ago, he had asthma, which could exacerbate the effects of both the natural gas and the chemicals added to give the gas a warning odor.

She herself was beginning to feel dizzy and tired, although how much was from the panic she was fighting and how much was the gas itself, she wasn't sure.

Suddenly she heard three loud bangs and froze,

terrified for a moment that the gas had already ignited. Only when the sounds came again did she recognize what they were. Someone was knocking on the door.

She stayed very still for a long moment, waiting for any sound from within the house that might reveal the presence of their captors, before she realized they wouldn't risk staying in a house full of gas. She closed the saw blade and felt her way to the closet door, banging on the wood and shouting. "We're in here. The place is full of gas! Help us!"

She wondered if anyone heard.

JESSE FOUND A SIDE PORCH on the alley side of the house, with a rickety screen door sagging on its hinges. It opened with a heart-stopping creak but created no sparks. Jesse stepped onto the small porch and took a look at the door to the inside. It was wood, with a flaked paint job, and had four panes of glass set into a cross frame in the top half of the door. Locked, he learned when he gave the doorknob a futile twist.

He pulled off his jacket and wrapped it around his arm. With a sharp jab of his elbow, he shattered the glass in the pane nearest to the doorknob. After using the jacket to clear off the jagged glass still poking out of the window frame, he reached through the opening and stretched his arm down until his fingers closed around the knob of the deadbolt lock.

No sparks, he prayed silently, and twisted the knob. It didn't move easily, but it moved, and he withdrew his arm and tried the door again.

It swung open, and the odor of gas hit him like a physical blow.

"I'm in!" he called to his cousin and Powell, but he didn't wait for them to show up before he walked into the small kitchen. Nor did he bother drawing his GLOCK—he didn't dare use it. He doubted any of the bad guys would have stuck around once they started the gas leak anyway. It was dangerous as hell just walking through the place, thanks to the volatile, highly explosive gas surrounding him.

"Evie?" he called.

Nearby, he heard a racking series of coughs. He followed the sound to a small door just off the kitchen. "Evie?" he called again.

"Not…Evie…." A male voice, punctuated by harsh coughs, came from behind the door.

"Is she in the house?"

"Think so."

Jesse squelched the urge to leave Endrex, or whoever it was behind this door, to his own devices and search for Evie instead. If this guy was Endrex, and he had the evidence General Ross had believed, he might be their only chance to bring down the Espera Group.

Just then Briggs and his partner, Caleb Lowell, came through the back door, saving him from having to choose. "Someone's in here, and he doesn't sound good. I have to go look for Evie."

"Go," Briggs said firmly, his dark eyes understanding.

Jesse went deeper into the house. "Evie?"

"Jesse!" The sound of Evie's voice, raspy but strong, nearly knocked Jesse's legs out from under him.

He followed her voice until he reached a small closet in the hallway near a tiny bathroom. "Evie, are you okay?"

"We've got to get out of here. They've set a gas leak—"

"I know. Let's try to unlock this door."

"I don't think there's any good way to do it without risking sparks. Go to the room to your right and try to cut through the plaster with your pocketknife or something. I'm nearly through my side of the wall."

He stared at the closed door a moment. "They let you keep a knife?"

Her low chuckle caught him by surprise. "Hid it in my bra. Kiss Megan for me when we get home."

He raced to the room next door, a small, empty bedroom unnaturally dark for that time of the afternoon, thanks to an overgrown boxwood outside the room's single window, blocking out daylight. He didn't risk turning on a light, fearful of striking sparks. He picked a spot on the wall next to the closet and pulled out his pocketknife. "Knock on the wall where you're cutting," he called.

He followed the series of raps until satisfied he was cutting in the right place. His saw blade made quick work of the chipped, cracked plaster wall, slicing a large square open in just a couple of minutes. Carefully pulling the chunks of plaster away, he looked inside the wall and, for a moment, saw only darkness.

Then Evie's small, oval face appeared in the opening, her eyes wide with a combination of fear and relief. "Get me out of here," she said in a whiskey-dark voice.

He caught her arms and pulled her through the opening he'd made, crushing her close. "Are you hurt?"

She wriggled free. "This place is a big old bomb waiting to go off. Let's get out of here!"

Grabbing her hand, he led the way out.

Chapter Nineteen

Jesse returned from the coffeepot on the far side of the waiting room with two cups full of hot, steaming wake-up juice to find Evie talking to a man wearing green scrubs. She looked relieved when the man walked away.

"Cav's out of the woods."

Cav, Jesse knew now, was Nolan Cavanaugh, the real name of the computer genius who went by Endrex online. General Marsh had called with that information shortly after he and Evie arrived at the hospital. Evie hadn't wanted to be checked out by the paramedics who'd arrived on the scene of the gas leak along with the fire department, but Jesse had insisted she let them take a look. To his relief, she'd been given a clean bill of health by the emergency medical techs.

"She'll want to go to the hospital with her friend," Jesse had warned his cousin Briggs when he and his partner looked inclined to take her to police headquarters for debriefing. "You can get her statement there."

And so he had, questioning her for almost an hour while they waited for word of Nolan Cavanaugh's condition. Evie had given Briggs a detailed description of both men, and the Birmingham Police Department had an APB out on both of them.

"We need to talk to Cav about his evidence," Evie said. "He never told me where he had it, and I have no idea if he told those men where it was. We can't let them destroy our best chance to stop the Espera Group."

"I'm not sure they're letting nonrelatives see him."

"I'll tell them I'm his sister. Who's going to check?"

As it turned out, they didn't have to tell anyone anything. Briggs came into the waiting room and motioned for Evie to join him. "Mr. Cavanaugh needs to talk to you."

"I'm coming, too," Jesse said, giving his cousin a look that warned against argument.

Briggs nodded and led them down the hall to the private room where the hospital staff had put Cavanaugh to recuperate from his exposure to the gas fumes.

He frowned at the sight of Jesse following Evie into the room. "Who are you?"

"Evie's boyfriend," Jesse answered flatly.

Evie's gaze whipped up to meet his. He silently

dared her to contradict him, a smile tickling the corner of his lips.

Her mouth curved in response as she turned to Cavanaugh. "Jesse Cooper, this is Cav. Cav, Jesse." She sat on the edge of the bed and took Cavanaugh's hand. "You scared me. I was terrified you weren't going to make it long enough for me to get out of that closet to help you."

"Me, too," he said with a weak grin. He leaned his head closer to hers. "I have what you're looking for. I trust you to do the right thing with it."

"Where is it?" she asked.

He bent closer and whispered something in her ear.

She sat back in surprise. "You're kidding."

He managed a weak smile. "It seemed to be the safest place."

"Where is it?" Jesse asked, trying not to sound as impatient as he felt.

Cavanaugh reached over to the bedside table and picked up a small plastic bag full of his personal items, things the E.R. staff had removed while they were working on him. He pulled out a gold ring with a blue stone and handed it to Evie. "Push the stone three times."

Evie did as told. After the third click, the stone setting popped open on a hinge. As Jesse stepped closer for a better look, Evie withdrew three tiny chips from the hollow compartment inside the ring.

"Everything's there. I pulled it from personal

computers, work computers, satellite transmissions—I've been on this for years, since I first heard about what the State Department did to Maddox Heller." Cavanaugh's hoarse voice dripped with indignation. "Total railroad job, and I wanted to prove it. Heller was my personal bodyguard during some work I did for the leathernecks before he was deployed to Kaziristan. Stand-up guy. But the deeper I looked, the more slime I found. It became about so much more than one good Marine being slandered."

"You should have told someone what you had."

"I did. I told General Ross. And you saw what happened to his son. And then to him."

Jesse had seen a lot of people suffer at the hands of the SSU and the people who paid their bills. "We'll get this to the right people."

"Call Blackledge." Cavanaugh grimaced. "General Ross told me the senator's a wily old bastard, but he plays it straight on stuff like this. He won't let this evidence disappear."

"We will." Evie squeezed his hand and let go. "You take care of yourself, okay? And you know where to find me."

Cavanaugh grinned at her. "With him?"

Evie turned to look at Jesse with bright, inquisitive eyes. "We'll see."

They stepped out of Cavanaugh's room and almost ran straight into Megan and Isabel. "We got here as soon as we could. Are you two okay?"

Jesse hugged his sisters. "We're good. And we have the evidence."

"Really?" Isabel's eyes widened. "On you?"

"Yes." He looked at Evie. "And we need to get it somewhere safe. We've all risked too much to let it slip out of our hands this time."

A QUIET BUT INTENSE Cooper family party commenced in the conference room at Cooper Security within an hour of their return. Jesse's brothers and sisters, and even a few cousins, showed up for the impromptu celebration, along with Evie's parents, her sister and her brother-in-law. After an emotional reunion with her family, Evie found herself handed from Cooper to Cooper for hugs and congratulations.

Even Rick's wife, Amanda, who was the most reserved and cautious of the Cooper family, gave Evie a fierce hug, with a laughing apology for her very pregnant belly getting in the way.

"You took a huge risk today," Amanda said softly, her eyes shining with understanding. She rubbed her stomach. "I hope everything you've done today makes the world a safer place for all of us."

Jesse had handed over the evidence chips to his brother Rick as soon as they arrived, telling him, "Put it in the safe at the alternate site." Evie had no idea where the alternate site might be, but she trusted Jesse knew what he was doing, at least where his work was concerned.

Where his heart was concerned, however, she was beginning to wonder if he had a clue. For a moment in Cav's room, when he'd called Evie his girlfriend and looked at her with such possessive passion in his dark eyes, she'd been sure he was on the verge of telling her he had realized she was the Marsh sister he really wanted. But once he'd run into his sisters at the hospital, he'd been all business, except for these few moments of family celebration he allowed himself.

But even that didn't last, as he quickly excused himself and headed out onto the terrace outside the conference room. As Evie watched, he pulled out his cell phone and made a call.

Evie couldn't wait any longer. She followed him outside, trying to keep enough distance that she didn't eavesdrop on his phone conversation. Even so, the terrace was small, and she made out enough of his end of the call to realize he was talking to Senator Gerald Blackledge, Alabama's savvy and experienced senior U.S. senator.

"Thank you, sir. I'll meet you in Montgomery tomorrow afternoon." Jesse said goodbye and hung up the phone, sticking it in the pocket of his jacket. He shot Evie a smile that made her heart shimmy. "Hell of a day."

She nodded, rubbing her arms as the cool evening air began to seep through her thin cardigan. "Do you think Cav's evidence is going to be enough?"

"Delilah and my cousin Troy just headed over to the alternate site to take a look. They've been running our SSU apprehension unit, so they know the most about the Espera Group and what they've been up to. They'll let us know what we have as soon as they take a look. But I think it must be pretty good. I don't think General Ross would have risked so much to protect something that was anything less than explosive."

"If only Cav weren't so paranoid. He could have given General Ross or someone the information a couple of years ago."

Jesse shrugged off his jacket and wrapped it around her shoulders, tugging her closer with the jacket's lapels. "I don't want to talk about your hacker boyfriend."

She arched an eyebrow and kept her voice light. "I thought you told Cav *you* were my boyfriend."

"I did, didn't I?" He smiled down at her, his arms sliding around her waist. "I suppose I forgot to consult you. I'm absentminded that way."

She lifted her chin. "A girl likes to be asked."

"So I hear." He leaned closer, his breath warm on her cheeks, smelling of peppermint and coffee. "The question is, what should I ask?"

"Can't help you there, big guy."

He threaded one hand through her hair, his palm settling against her cheek. "You're going to make me walk out here on this shaky limb all by myself?"

"Maybe it's not all that shaky."

"Evie Marsh, I think I love you."

Her heart skipped a beat, but she maintained her cool. "Think?"

He smiled. "Okay, I know. I love you. Beyond all sense."

"Because it's not sensible to love me?" she said, feigning seriousness even though her heart was soaring toward the stars glittering overhead.

"Because I love you until I'm utterly senseless," he countered, brushing his mouth across her brow. "Because I've been falling in love with you since you were seventeen years old and I was still chasing your sister, only it took me until now to realize it was happening. If that's not senseless, I don't know what is." He dropped kisses down her temple and over her cheek, moving inexorably closer to her mouth.

"How about falling in love with your sister's fiancé and staying that way for ten years without any reason to hope for his love in return?" she whispered as his lips brushed over hers.

He pulled back, staring down at her with a frown. "Ten years?"

"Senseless," she said with a sigh.

He cradled her face between his hands. "So we'll be senseless together."

"That sounds sensible," she said, lifting her face for a kiss.

Epilogue

On December 18, in the middle of a Cooper Security video conference with the U.S. attorney in charge of the widespread investigation into After-Assets, the Espera Group, and over a dozen politicians, lobbyists and executive branch staffers, Amanda Cooper's water broke.

Jesse put the U.S. attorney on hold and turned to Rick, who was looking comically panic-stricken as he tried to help his wife deal with the mess. "Just go, Rick. Get her to the hospital and have that baby. We'll handle this."

As his sister Megan and her husband stepped in to clean up, Jesse adjusted the webcam to hide their activity and resumed the conference, trying not to hurry the U.S. attorney off. The energy in the room had changed with the onset of Amanda's labor. Their baby would be the first Cooper grandchild in their branch of the family, and every Cooper in the conference room was nearly as excited as Rick had been.

The U.S. attorney, Laura Pelham, looked impatient when her image reappeared on the screen. "Is this a bad time?"

"No, sorry. We had a brief interruption, but we're back. Has there been any progress in apprehending the fugitive AfterAssets operatives?"

"We've rounded up about two dozen, but based on the information Nolan Cavanaugh managed to archive, we think there are at least twenty more operatives. Apparently they expanded their personnel beyond the original twenty-three Special Service Unit members MacLear employed."

"Is Cavanaugh in protective custody?" Evie asked.

"Yes. He's safe. A bit hard to handle, but safe."

Jesse smiled at Evie before turning back to Pelham. "Anything Cooper Security can do to help out, you let us know."

"Will do," Pelham promised. "But don't assume all the danger is over, Mr. Cooper. There are still people out there who might see you and your company as an obstacle."

There always were, Jesse thought.

He ended the conference call and turned to look at the others gathered around the table. Most of them were his brothers and sisters, including Wade, who was back after nearly three months of guard duty protecting Annie Harlowe and her family. He and Annie were engaged, planning a quick and stress-free wedding after the first of the year. Quick and stress-free was turning out to be a Cooper family tradition for weddings; just last week, Shannon and Gideon had taken a long weekend in Gatlinburg, Tennessee, and returned to surprise the family with their wedding license and a pair of carved stone rings they'd bought for wedding bands.

"Can we go to the hospital now?" Isabel broke the silence.

"Go," Jesse said with a laugh, waving them toward the door. "We have a new Cooper to welcome into the world."

He caught Evie's hand as she started out after the others, drawing her back to the table.

She turned to look at him, a quizzical expression in her blue eyes. "Aren't we going to the hospital, too?"

"In a minute." He stood and tugged her into his arms. "I've been thinking about us."

Her brow creased. "Is that good or bad?"

"Good, I hope." He briefly considered going down on one knee, old-style, but decided to just say what he wanted to say straight-out. No fuss, no flowery words. That wasn't how he and Evie operated. "I think we should get married."

Her lips quirked. "You think so?"

He smiled back. "You don't?"

"No, of course I do. I just remembered the elaborate way you proposed to Rita."

"But you're not Rita." He cradled her face between his hands. "And I'm not that man anymore. You and I don't need the silly trappings, do we?"

She shook her head. "I love you. I know you love me."

"I do, you know. More than anything in this life."

She brushed her lips against his. "Can we elope like everyone else did? And really soon?"

He laughed. "Mind reader."

"But first you have a niece or nephew to meet." Evie pulled away and tugged his hand, leading him toward the door.

"Wait." He stopped just outside in the corridor. "I may not be the most traditional fiancé in the world, but I did remember the ring." He pulled the small velvet box from his jacket pocket, where it had been burning a hole all day. He opened it to reveal a slim gold band with a square-cut sapphire flanked by diamonds. "It reminded me of your eyes."

She gazed up at him with those bright blue eyes, grinning with delight. "It's amazing."

"So, yes?"

"Yes." She hugged him fiercely. "When?"

"How about Christmas? So I'll never forget our anniversary."

"Lazy, Cooper. Very lazy." Laughing, she kissed him, pushing him against the wall of the corridor.

By the time they made it to the hospital, much, much later, Audrey Jane Cooper had emerged, red-faced and screaming, into the world. A world, Jesse hoped as he watched his brother and sister-in-law cradle their newborn, just a little bit safer today than three months ago.

But not safe enough.

Never safe enough.

*   *   *   *   *

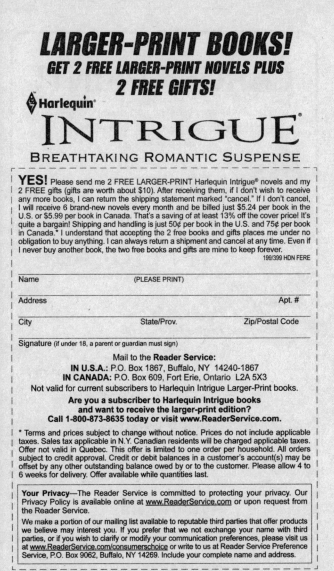

LARGER-PRINT BOOKS!
GET 2 FREE LARGER-PRINT NOVELS PLUS
2 FREE GIFTS!

❖ Harlequin®

INTRIGUE®

BREATHTAKING ROMANTIC SUSPENSE

YES! Please send me 2 FREE LARGER-PRINT Harlequin Intrigue® novels and my 2 FREE gifts (gifts are worth about $10). After receiving them, if I don't wish to receive any more books, I can return the shipping statement marked "cancel." If I don't cancel, I will receive 6 brand-new novels every month and be billed just $5.24 per book in the U.S. or $5.99 per book in Canada. That's a saving of at least 13% off the cover price! It's quite a bargain! Shipping and handling is just 50¢ per book in the U.S. and 75¢ per book in Canada.* I understand that accepting the 2 free books and gifts places me under no obligation to buy anything. I can always return a shipment and cancel at any time. Even if I never buy another book, the two free books and gifts are mine to keep forever.

199/399 HDN FERE

Name	(PLEASE PRINT)	
Address		Apt. #
City	State/Prov.	Zip/Postal Code

Signature (if under 18, a parent or guardian must sign)

Mail to the **Reader Service:**
IN U.S.A.: P.O. Box 1867, Buffalo, NY 14240-1867
IN CANADA: P.O. Box 609, Fort Erie, Ontario L2A 5X3

Not valid for current subscribers to Harlequin Intrigue Larger-Print books.

**Are you a subscriber to Harlequin Intrigue books
and want to receive the larger-print edition?
Call 1-800-873-8635 today or visit www.ReaderService.com.**

* Terms and prices subject to change without notice. Prices do not include applicable taxes. Sales tax applicable in N.Y. Canadian residents will be charged applicable taxes. Offer not valid in Quebec. This offer is limited to one order per household. All orders subject to credit approval. Credit or debit balances in a customer's account(s) may be offset by any other outstanding balance owed by or to the customer. Please allow 4 to 6 weeks for delivery. Offer available while quantities last.

Your Privacy—The Reader Service is committed to protecting your privacy. Our Privacy Policy is available online at www.ReaderService.com or upon request from the Reader Service.

We make a portion of our mailing list available to reputable third parties that offer products we believe may interest you. If you prefer that we not exchange your name with third parties, or if you wish to clarify or modify your communication preferences, please visit us at www.ReaderService.com/consumerchoice or write to us at Reader Service Preference Service, P.O. Box 9062, Buffalo, NY 14269. Include your complete name and address.

HILP11B

FAMOUS FAMILIES

YES! Please send me the *Famous Families* collection featuring the Fortunes, the Bravos, the McCabes and the Cavanaughs. This collection will begin with 3 FREE BOOKS and 2 FREE GIFTS in my very first shipment— and more valuable free gifts will follow! My books will arrive in 8 monthly shipments until I have the entire 51-book *Famous Families* collection. I will receive 2-3 free books in each shipment and I will pay just $4.49 U.S./$5.39 CDN for each of the other 4 books in each shipment, plus $2.99 for shipping and handling.* If I decide to keep the entire collection, I'll only have paid for 32 books because 19 books are free. I understand that accepting the 3 free books and gifts places me under no obligation to buy anything. I can always return a shipment and cancel at any time. My free books and gifts are mine to keep no matter what I decide.

268 HCN 0387   468 HCN 0387

Name _____ (PLEASE PRINT) _____

Address _____ Apt. # _____

City _____ State/Prov. _____ Zip/Postal Code _____

Signature (if under 18, a parent or guardian must sign) _____

Mail to the **Reader Service:**

IN U.S.A.: P.O. Box 1867, Buffalo, NY 14240-1867
IN CANADA: P.O. Box 609, Fort Erie, Ontario L2A 5X3

ReaderService.com

Manage your account online!

- Review your order history
- Manage your payments
- Update your address

**We've designed
the Reader Service website
just for you.**

Enjoy all the features!

- Reader excerpts from any series
- Respond to mailings and special monthly offers
- Discover new series available to you
- Browse the Bonus Bucks catalogue
- Share your feedback

Visit us at:

ReaderService.com

RS12